Arlene Mighton began her writing career while nursing in California. Upon returning to Canada to retire, she took up writing full-time as a hobby. She joined a writer's group called Writer's Ink and, after one year, began the process towards publication. Previously, she worked in Montreal and was associated with the organization Canadian Culturama Programs, a non-profit organization promoting Canadian authors. She will soon be completing her Bachelor of English at the UofS. She likes to travel, work-out, and go to galleries.

To Dorrie Manu – Thank you for your sharp insights while proofreading the book.

To Mark Malatesta – Thank you for encouraging me to publish in the New York market.

To my parents, Adella and Melvin Mighton – Thank you, from your loving daughter.

Arlene Mighton

BEN OF NIGGLEWOOD

AUSTIN MACAULEY PUBLISHERS™

LONDON • CAMBRIDGE • NEW YORK • SHARJAH

Ordering Information
Quantity sales: Special discounts are available on quantity purchases by corporations, associations, and others. For details, contact the publisher at the address below.

Publisher's Cataloging-in-Publication data
Mighton, Arlene
Ben of Nigglewood

ISBN 9798889101581 (Paperback)
ISBN 9798889103899 (ePub e-book)

Library of Congress Control Number: 2024902095

www.austinmacauley.com/us

First Published 2024
Austin Macauley Publishers LLC
40 Wall Street, 33rd Floor, Suite 3302
New York, NY 10005
USA

mail-usa@austinmacauley.com
+1 (646) 5125767

I would like to thank the ladies of Writer's Ink for their invaluable time and effort in critiquing the book. Also, I would like to thank Dorrie R. Manu for her sharp insights while proofreading the text. Many thanks to Dr. Barb Langhorst for her encouragement to the end. And thanks to Ben List and the staff of Austin Macauley Publishers for 'picking up the book' and deeming it worthwhile to publish.

Table of Contents

Chapter 1
Nigglewood Convalescent Manor

Nigglewood Convalescent Manor was situated at the corner of Lundy and Twenty-Sixth street in Los Angeles, opposite a thriving marketplace, kitty corner to a local bakery and fast-food chain, and adjacent to a lush green park, boasting of exotic plants and a colorful array of birds. In the center of the park was a fishpond surrounded by small bushes. The owner was a fifty-year-old-man named John Nigglewood, who had purchased the property in the seventies and was rumored to have shady connections in his business dealings.

The clientele that came to reside at Nigglewood emerged from all walks of life, and reality had left an indelible imprint on each one. Some had been homeless, others – abandoned by family members, and still others, victims of drug abuse and small, petty crimes. For those ailing in health, the manor provided a hospice. Individuals who had taken to the streets – that is to say, to beg or steal – found acceptance and refuge in the pink stucco two-story building. Patients recovering from a malady in the hospital were sent there on occasion before returning to the community. Highlights for the inhabitant were to spend several hours a day on the balcony socializing over a cigarette or playing frequent visits to a friendly receptionist who handled daily mail and phone calls at the front desk.

One of the residents, a tall, stocky, well-built man wearing a tattered green plaid jacket, black overalls and rubber boots lumbered past the well-polished, dark brown reception desk. On this particular day, he stopped for a moment, hoping to flirt with the young lady on duty. He winked at the receptionist who was at the computer and lifted his red wool cap to greet her.

"Hello, Carolina. Good to see you. I feel the black cloud is lifting over Nigglewood. I don't see the local slammers or them housing authorities around here lately. All the fraud and abuse a thing of the past?" he asked softly.

The receptionist closed the computer and looked up at him with a sparkle in her eyes.

"After considerable struggle, Mr. Cleaver, the manor has finally cleared its name. Opened its doors with some hesitation, though. I just booked the last room. No one cares about scandal, theft, or fraud. All that matters are three scales meals a day and a roof over one's head. Right, my good man?"

Cleaver nodded his head with approval.

"You got that right. Now, I must see someone in room 112. Nice talking to you."

He shuffled down the corridor until he reached the room. The door was slightly ajar, and he nudged it with one foot. It gave without resistance.

He thought out loud, "That could be dangerous. Old Ben better get that fixed."

He poked his head around the door and spoke in a gruff manner: "Heh, big Ben, your breakfast is sitting outside the room on the floor. If you don't eat soon, the tray will be covered with dust. Better grab it before the cleaning lady tosses it."

A very overweight man of about fifty-five years sat quietly at a window looking at the rose bushes. He turned the wheelchair slowly around with a still-functional right hand and faced Cleaver. His entire left side slumped sideways, with the arm dangling over the side. His left leg and foot lay motionless on a footrest. An old brown Fedora hat lay to one side of his head, and he wore a dark green jacket over a yellow plaid shirt. Khaki trousers and black shoes with well-worn heels gave him an air of simplicity. Ben Walker had not showered for several days, and this caused a slight whiff of body odor from time to time when he raised the right arm.

He gave a hoarse laugh, then answered in a slightly slurred speech; "The house staff left it there because I complained about the food yesterday, Mr. Cleaver. That's my punishment. Indeed, they know how to retaliate. If some kind soul doesn't have mercy on me, the tray will remain on the floor. At least I can still feed myself with my right hand. Without this independence, life would be completely unbearable. That's the positive side to this terrible experience."

Ben glanced at the tray near the door way.

"Look at that disgusting food. Shove the tray aside, and close the door, mate. Let them trip on it."

With that, Ben swung around to the window again and nuzzled his face against it. It was half open, and a cool breeze wafted in from the outside. It had a soothing effect on him, and he gazed into the distance, hypnotized by the sparkling sun and azure sky. He wiped beads of perspiration from his forehead with a chubby black hand.

After a brief moment of silence, his friend spoke up, "Your room is a sight to behold, my good man. Are they boycotting your maid service, too?"

Ben grunted loudly, and his body seemed to shake like a bowl of jelly.

"I complained about that three days ago. They haven't changed my linen since last week, and my garbage is still piled high in the waste bin. They're lucky this kind soul still goes to the bathroom. Just think of the mess if urine and feces were everywhere. Then the house staff would have to clean this despicable hole. You notice how certain individuals have their rooms cleaned around here?"

A gloomy, unpleasant feeling surfaced, and Ben had a compulsion to hit the windowpane. As he raised his right arm, he lost balance in the chair, and the impact of the blow was displaced on to the window frame, causing the glass to shimmy. He stared at the windowpane, then started to giggle nervously.

"The line between black and white is so clearly demarcated. It's all in the color, man. Have you ever imagined what it would be like to have white skin? Think of the privileges you'd have. Why, the entire world would be a footstool before you, dear friend."

Cleaver held up a fat, flabby black arm and placed an index finger on his lower, bulbous lip.

Then he spoke gingerly while strutting around the room: "That's enough, my friend. I don't want to hear anymore. Thank the lord for small mercies at Nigglewood. At least you have a place to rest that weary head of yours. Beat them at their game, Ben. Go out into the community and hire a maid to clean your room and do some laundry. Such an action will create an uproar among the attendants, and old Nigglewood will be hopping. Here, let me give you some help towards the cause."

Cleaver withdrew a twenty and a ten dollars' bill from a black and gold leather wallet and placed them in his lap. Ben fingered the paper bills for a few moments, then tossed them onto the floor.

"Keep your money. Give it to some guttersnipe who is desperate for cash. There are plenty of those at Nigglewood. The maids would definitely be jealous of your charity, and matters may become worse for you. I have my own scheme to get back at them."

There was laughter somewhere in the corridor now, and both men took to silence. When the noise passed, Ben placed his right hand over his face and sobbed into a tissue. He was not as tough as everyone thought.

At length, he blurted out his words with difficulty, fighting back the tears; "Cleaver, Cleaver, it's, it's …"

The tears flowed down his left sagging cheek.

"It's a shame life has dealt us such a painful blow. My mother would be horrified if she saw me like this. A letter was posted yesterday telling her all was well at Nigglewood and that this place was a real haven of rest. If only she knew …"

For a short period of time, neither of them spoke, and all that could be heard was the ticking of the clock in the background. Cleaver moved quietly to the forlorn soul, placed his arm around him and massaged his scalp with the other hand. He shook his head in dismay. Nothing seemed to cheer his friend.

At length, Ben gave a big sigh and spoke, "My life is but a breath, and my sojourn here on Earth is of little importance. Even as a businessman, the pleasure was short lived. At one time, I lived well – made thousands of dollars, owned fancy houses, traveled around the world, socialized with people in high places, was loved by my wife and daughter. When my business went bankrupt, all quality of living deteriorated along with my assets. My wife divorced me, and living became futile."

A puzzled look appeared on Cleaver's face.

"What about your daughter, Lise? When did you last hear from her?"

The mere mention of Lise's name caused Ben to flinch, and his face became red and sweaty, his eyes fierce and angry.

His body quivered as he continued: "My ex-wife has complete control over my daughter. When my business went belly-up, she poisoned my daughter's mind with all sorts of insults about me. The last time I saw Lise was four years ago during Christmas break in New Hampshire. My ex-wife, at that time felt, I had been a supportive father and agreed to the two of us meeting on Christmas Day. We exchanged stockings, ate a scrumptious meal, and watched television most of the afternoon. See the stocking on top of the mirror? That was her gift to me. It was filled with all sorts of goodies – candy, cigarettes, men's cologne, a pen, and a pair of red socks. The card had love and kisses written all over it."

For a moment, Ben slipped into a dreamy state as he pondered his daughter, and his mind went back to the festive celebration four years ago. He closed his eyes and recalled their dialogue together that afternoon. No words or thoughts could match the joy he felt at that time.

When he came out of the daze, he spoke up: "I put the stocking on the mirror so I would be reminded of my darling every day. Alas! Such moments are short lived. The visits and calls are no more. The last time I spoke to my beloved Lise, on the phone, was two years ago. She told me I was a terrible dad, irresponsible, a drunk, and a lowlife. Now, all I have left is my mother. At least she still calls me once or twice a year to tell me how much she loves me."

Ben held up his right arm and sobbed into his shirt's sleeve. Cleaver cradled him in his arms, gently caressing and rocking him back and forth.

Finally, he sounded off: "I care about you, old boy. Let's go out for the afternoon. There's a sale on at DepBurn's department store. Maybe, just maybe, we'll be lucky. Sometimes they raffle baskets of food and give away money – and there are lots of pretty ladies shopping there. Who knows, maybe we can snort a little cocaine if a dealer comes our way."

Ben pushed Cleaver back, released the brake of his wheelchair, and proceeded at a slow speed to the center of the room.

"I'm not in the mood for department stores. That type of rendezvous is for mothers, children, and pretty young ladies who want to show their tops and bottoms. Why don't you take old Nigglewood with you? Our scandalous owner could use a boost in self-esteem. Don't think he ever recovered from his seventies scandal of embezzling funds and tax evasion."

Ben gave a cold, sardonic laugh and continued, his eyebrows twitching slightly, his eyeballs bulging from their sockets.

"Old Nigglewood escaped a potential scandal by the skin of his teeth several weeks ago. I was resting on the top of my bed when the scumbag quietly entered the room and tried to grope me. I guess he wanted to add me to his list of damned old ghouls. I gave him a punch with my good hand in the face and sent him flying. His mouth was cut and bleeding. He shook his fist at me and threatened with a kick. There was to be no squealing on him, or he would retaliate. I haven't, and neither will you, Cleaver."

Ben nervously moved his chair back and forth, eyeing his friend in front of him. Cleaver was nonplussed by his tale, and felt a huge lump swell in his throat. He swallowed hard, and eventually, it passed.

Finally, he spoke: "You know I won't betray confidences, my friend. Your secret is hid in my heart forever. However, if someone else finds out about your harassment and it goes public, we'll be out on the street begging for mercy and lodging. To move to another place would be disastrous. Our disability checks would be gone in no time. BacNauld's Bar and Grill would be history. No more of that blond-haired hottie; Fifi."

There was an uneasy atmosphere now, and Ben's buddy gave a furtive glance around the room.

Finally, he placed his lips on his friend's ear and whispered, "I don't think you should have divulged your secret here. Look at the cracks in the wall. Besides, there's a hole above the sink. Someone could have overheard everything."

Ben was startled by his friend's observations and retorted, "Quiet! I've had enough of your chatter. You're just like them magpies outdoors. Always cawing."

He glanced at his watch and noticed it was almost eleven o'clock.

"Oh! My buxom sweetheart with her brown-black mink eyelashes, plunging neckline, and blue miniskirt with those plump legs will be finishing her shift soon. She'll definitely be looking for me and wondering where I am. I'm off to the grill. So long, friend."

Ben steered his wheelchair into the center of the room, and paused before the mirror for one last inspection. He fluffed his tangled hair with the good hand, then sprayed some outdated men's cologne onto his neck and jacket. A sharp, stale odor pierced the air, and the two men coughed for several minutes.

Then he winked at his reflection in the mirror and spoke jestingly to it: "You don't look too bad for an old cripple. I must be on my way now. Hunger pangs are gnawing. Maybe you'd like to join me at BacNauld's Bar and Grill? My waitress Fifi will be serving me, and I'm sure she'd be delighted to meet you. How about it, old chap?"

Ben slapped his thigh and laughed.

"I don't think you're too interested. I'll see you later and tell you all about it."

For an instant, the reflection trembled, and a sinister look appeared on his face. Then he rolled up his shirtsleeves and crossed both arms in a very angry look. The image furrowed both brows, and suddenly reached for Ben's right arm. On impulse, Ben pulled back and quickly put the chair in reverse.

"Did you see that, Cleaver? The mirror image became a person and tried to touch me. Has Nigglewood become a den of demons?"

Just then, the PA system announced a general inspection of Nigglewood convalescent and all occupants were to be out of their rooms.

"Come on, Cleaver, let's get moving."

Ben paused at the door, then turned the chair slowly around to face his friend one last time.

"You have a lot of gall talking about Fifi. What about your sweetie, Cassey Bromhedge from Derby, England? Sad lassie she is. No better than us. At least she has a small apartment and some privacy. I'll give her that. Have you seen your lowlife, lately?"

"Enough of your idle talk, man. Turn down the tone of your voice and get moving. My, you're noisy today."

Loud voices were heard now down below, and doors began to open and bang shut.

"That's the inspectors. Let's get out of here before they arrive," cried Ben.

As the wheelchair rolled toward the door, Ben felt a surge of energy and gave a strong kick against the doorknob. The door collided against the outside wall with a loud bang, and the impact echoed down the hallway. He rolled from side to side down the corridor and maneuvered around several breakfast trays lying on the floor. Accidentally, he drove over an unopened package near the stairwell. Glass broke, and raspberry jam oozed from every corner.

Once he arrived at the elevators, he shouted down the dimly lit passageway: "Why don't you join me at BacNauld's for a late breakfast? Fifi's friend Sally Mae is working today. She is a dolly bird! Has a mermaid tattoo on her back, the fish tail descending to her bottom. The bar staff have nicknamed her 'Mermaid Sally' because she can wiggle her tailbone just like them fishes. I'd check her out."

The provocation was too much for Cleaver. He stormed down the hallway like an angry bear. As he approached the wheelchair, he pushed one side into the wall.

"There – enough from you and the BacNauld women. Your Fifi is certainly no saint. About a month ago, I had lunch at the grill, and three truckers were placing their orders with the 'lunch-in' girl. One of them truckers snuggled up to Fifi, pinched her bottom, then planted a kiss on her neck. You could smell Fifi's perfume on him every time you passed their table. And you want to savor a hamburger from a woman like that?"

"That's none of your damn business," growled Ben. "Now let my chair go this minute. If you're not at BacNauld's Bar in a half hour, I'll take it you're not coming. I'll see you later this evening."

"Don't sit on the outdoor terrace all day drinking coffee and smoking cigarettes. Make yourself useful. So long, comrade."

As soon as Ben was outside Nigglewood, he took to the street like a Trojan. Gradually, the convalescent home became a blur in the distance, and Ben began to breathe a sigh of relief. At last, there was some reprieve from his woes, and he sped on.

Chapter 2
BacNauld's Bar and Grill

The wheelchair bearing its occupant sped along the sidewalk, and rolled through two yellow lights just in the nick of time. His heart fluttered as the oncoming traffic accelerated before the light turned green. A motorbike rounded a corner and clipped the chair's left brake, knocking the American flag attached to it into Ben's arm. The young cyclist maneuvered his bike into the next lane and opened the throttle as he sped away. Mr. Walker was nonchalant about these close calls, but he shuddered at the thought of a passerby helping him through an intersection if his strength failed or if the wheelchair became nonfunctional. How vulnerable the plight of the helpless could be!

The independence to come and go from Nigglewood Convalescent gave him great satisfaction, and he counted it a privilege to travel the walkway at his own volition. Occasionally, he had met fellow lodgers several miles away from the convalescent home, unable to wheel back to Lundy and Twenty-Sixth street because of fatigue or exhaustion. Those poor dear ones! They were at the mercy of a compassionate pedestrian. Certainly, it was a civic duty to press the walk button on their behalf, escort them across the street, and secure their chairs on a bus. Ben felt angst in his soul for them, and undergirded their free spirit to roll down the sidewalk, enjoy the cool breeze, smell the aroma of flowers, and rest under the branches of an old poplar tree. He stopped his chair for a moment, closed his eyes, and offered a prayer of thanks that his strength was still intact.

Nigglewood Convalescent was now completely out of sight, and the happy wanderer focused his attention on a very new and prosperous business section in the city, the Delta Commons. The Commons was very successful, and its bigness lured young and old alike. Ben felt his spirits lift as wonder and amazement seized him. There were pet shelters, quaint flower shops, elegant ladies apparel stores, a shop with designer hats and men's sport wear, pharmacies boasting herbal medicines from China, a barbershop with a rapid rotating red, white, and blue light, moving so fast, Ben got dizzy watching it. Numerous eateries began to appear, and the scents of curry, bread making, and pastries stirred his sense of smell and caused continuous roiling from the stomach.

He stopped briefly to watch a chef make a batch of onion bagels. A server tossed him a fresh bagel and offered the thirsty soul a cup of fresh gourmet coffee–hazelnut toffee, no less. Ben paused at a Japanese sushi vendor on the street and curiosity held him. A cook gave him a rice patty filled with shrimp and avocados and a small cup of green tea. On, he rolled and came to a well-known restaurant named Brazen Lips. A chef was barbecuing on an open fire, and the scent of cooked chicken, beef, and pork caused a complete obsession for eating. With food in mind, Mr. Walker maneuvered the chair into the center of the sidewalk and wheeled ahead.

BacNauld's Bar and Grill suddenly appeared, and Ben turned the wheelchair into the inner aspect of the sidewalk, then rolled up the ramp for the handicapped. He pressed a button and instantly, the doors opened. Ben immediately entered the dining area and looked for a vacant table. His eyes fell on Fifi, in a far corner, taking orders from three boisterous truckers who had just stopped to eat at the grill. The three revelers were boasting about their Big Mac truck hauling tons of oil across North America and their safe arrival to various destinations. One trucker bragged about how punctual they were and how adept their driving skills had been in the safe handling of the oil.

Eyeing the three rogues suspiciously, Ben smiled icily with his lips and grunted with disgust. Then he secured the wheels of his chair at one table near the window and waited impatiently for Fifi to catch his attention. The pleasingly plump thirty-five-year-old was in no hurry today, and was passing the time joking with the three truckers while taking orders. Waves of jealousy passed through Ben, and he postured like a cat. He scowled and screwed his mouth to one side and became increasingly impatient with Fifi. Couldn't she at least turn for one minute from those bums and give this faithful customer some attention? Frustrated and hungry, he picked up a fork and gave it several knocks against a water glass in front of him.

Fifi half turned to see where the noise was coming from. As soon as she eyed Ben with the fork, she quickly turned her head and continued flirting with the truckers. Ben was furious and gave the glass a few more knocks with the fork. Then he raised his right arm in the air and cried out, "Away with them," in a loud voice that rang throughout the entire bar.

One of the truckers, a middle-aged man, wearing a brown cowboy hat, tight-fitting black jeans, and a brilliant blue T-shirt with copper accouterments, yelled out for the hungry and restless man to be quiet and wait his turn. Then he grabbed Fifi and pulled her to his lap. The trucker glanced over at Ben and was somewhat perturbed.

"Say, lady, you have an impatient customer over there by the window. He better mind his own business and wait his turn, or I'll show him a thing or two."

Fifi shivered slightly and goosebumps appeared on both arms. Quickly, she pinched the Texan's cheeks lightly and teased him:

"Don't mind him, Tiny Tim. He's harmless as a dove and a regular here. Rolls in at eleven o'clock sharp every day. Says good food is sadly lacking at Nigglewood Convalescent, his home. Have a little mercy for the less fortunate, my good man."

Another trucker named Bulldog Thornton felt a wave of compassion ripple through him, pulled out two twenty dollar bills from a snakeskin wallet, and handed them to Fifi.

"Honey pie, I don't like seeing the unfortunate suffer. A man needs to eat. If his dwelling place ain't giving him proper food, that, I dare say, is a crime worthy of an investigation. That makes me angry inside."

His black eyes glittered in the light, and beads of perspiration came and went on both eyebrows. Suddenly, the Bulldog stood up, pounded both fists against the chair, and then sat down again. The brief pummeling of the chair was enough to catch Ben's attention, and he sat back, mesmerized by the well-built trucker.

Indeed, Bulldog Thornton was a paragon of fitness and prided himself in wearing eye-catching apparel. A very expensive handmade, red, buckskin jacket fit snugly around his hips and waistline, and semiprecious stones and silver decorated the sleeves and the back. His feet were shod with a pair of custom-made black ostrich boots with mink lining, and the tips of the boots were trimmed with silver. He sported a dark-green felt hat with a pheasant's feather perched on one side. The hat accented his lean, muscular face, and his dark eyes sparkled under its brim. In short, the man was very handsome, robust in health, and very energetic.

Fifi took the two twenty-dollar bills, fluttered her long mink eyelashes, and then spoke up somewhat irritated over the chair pounding: "Bulldog Thornton, thanks so much for the kind gesture. Now you just sit quiet, my dear friend, and don't pound that chair again with those mighty fists of yours. If the chair breaks with another pounding, the manager will be very upset."

The third trucker, a younger man with auburn hair, a salt and pepper goatee, flecked with red, gray-blue hazy eyes, and plump ruddy-colored cheeks, sat back quietly, listening to the entire commotion at hand. Becoming restless due to hunger pangs, he grabbed the table knife and tapped his protruding abdomen in time to the music.

Then he stretched out his muscular stout legs under the table, and placed his arms momentarily behind his head. Feeling in the mood for some jest, he crumpled a napkin and threw it Ben's way. The former businessman giggled at the daring gesture, grabbed the napkin as it neared his eyes, and poised to throw it back at him. At that point, Fifi, bashed and nettled, piped up:

"That isn't the answer, Mr. Ben. You're both guests at BacNauld's Bar, so no napkin throwing at each other. It's impolite and costly because you are wasting our napkins."

"He started it, Fifi." Ben sneered. "I'm just protecting myself. I come here for peace and quiet and a good square meal, and look what happens. Harassment by some roughneck I've never seen before."

Alaska Red, as the trucker was known, was annoyed by the remark but sat quietly, slurping his pint of beer. Finally, he burst forth and called to Ben in a thick, raspy voice:

"Heh, Mr. Nigglewood, Mr. Ben for short. That's some two-wheeler you ride about in. I suppose the green garbage bag over the back of the chair acts as a windbreaker. And those American flags on each side of the brakes they seem half-mast, but I must say, 'How patriotic!' Can't get any better than that! What's the fastest speed you can crank out with those wheels?"

The other two truckers burst out laughing and gave a toast to Alaska Red. Then, Tiny Tim jumped up and was about to vex Ben when he suffered a human moment: he belched gas from his mouth and burped loudly. Then he quickly grabbed his hat and placed it over his buttocks to muffle the passing of gas down below.

Ben reeled with anger at both men and was very irritated with them. He pounded his right fist on the table, then sternly replied to Alaska Red first in a sharp voice:

"My wheelchair is none of your business, Redhead. I can go faster with my chair than you can in that Green Mac of yours. Your truck is the size of an ox and probably climbs up a hill like a turtle. I can make a steep incline in ten minutes or less."

Then turning to Tiny Tim, a sarcastic expression flashed over his face, and he shouted out loud, with a blistering remark:

"And you, Mr. Gasman, your manners are disgusting. You owe us an apology for such crass behavior. There's a terrible smell in the room now, and we need to open some windows to air out the place."

Alaska Red grabbed his cowboy hat from the table, plunked in it on his head, and pushed Tiny Tim aside. He had an intense desire to suffocate Ben with his hands and lumbered chary toward the derelict.

Ben cringed in the chair with overwhelming fear, and pushed it against one wall near the door. His heart began to pound rapidly, and he felt slightly short of breath. He clenched his sanguine fist and braced for the worst.

Alaska Red felt ebullient for the moment and greeted various guests while he made his way to the helpless man. He stopped a few feet from Ben's table and decided to start with a gentle tutelage.

"Heh, Mr. Smartie – you've seen my green Mac outside, and judging from your comments, you're as jealous as a cat that it ain't yours. Look at the silver chrome on the side and how it shines in the sun. That wonderful truck motored through the western United States, up into Canada, and across the Northern Frontier, along the Alaska Highway, and finally down to Los Angeles, California. Essential goods and food products were delivered along the way. I must say that truck roared down the West Coast like a lion, and no vehicle ventured its way. It climbs a hill like a bear and can bump a useless vehicle out of the way in seconds. Your two-wheeler would be scrap metal if Big Mac thumped it from behind."

Ben froze in his chair and was speechless now. Try as he may, the words did not come forth. After several minutes, he was able to clear his throat and was about to speak when Tiny Tim gave a shout and lifted Fifi in the air and eventually, set her down in a chair. He decided to attend to the two men who were still arguing and walked over toward them.

"Gentlemen, please." He parlayed. "This is no way to behave or speak in front of a lady. Now let's have something more respectful and eloquent from both of you. Alaska Red – you like to recite cowboy poetry? Let's have some rhymes or jingles. It's much better than picking a fight or arguing with that bum. And Mr. Ben – let's have some decency from you. No more clicking the water glass with the fork. What you need is a dash of patience and some respect for Fifi. When she's finished with us, she'll take your order."

Tiny Tim sauntered over to Fifi, gently lifted her from the chair again, and set her down on his leg. She fanned her legs for support and placed a plump arm around the cowboy's neck and completed the order. Slyly, she glanced at Ben and could see he was fuming. This stirred her emotions even more, and she laughed heartily each time Tiny Tim told her a small joke. Ben cowered in the corner and gritted his teeth. His lips twitched with fiery indignation, and he sat silently, wondering what he should do. Glancing around the room, he noticed a young woman in her early twenties sitting at a small circular table by herself. Her table was littered with empty soda pop bottles, a courtesy of four young disheveled lads with spiked hairdos of red, purple, or green. Soon Ben was lost in admiration for such a beautiful creature and stared at her with intense delight.

The damsel who was named Meredith had long, fluffy black hair, thick black eyelashes, and bright ruby-red cheeks. Her brilliant green eyes sparkled in the light, and her slender arms and waist gave her an air of delicacy. She wore a bright-yellow sequined top and tight black leather pants that squeaked when she shifted in the chair. Around her waist, hung a black chain belt. Every time she took a drink, the belt made the noise of a jingle bell. Her fingernails and toenails were painted a bright red with flecks of gold. White chandelier earrings adorned her ears.

Ben Walker was taken by the joviality at hand and decided to join in. Knowing this would certainly agitate Fifi, he raised his right arm and beckoned to the bartender.

With uncontrollable laughter, he shouted loud, "A big Ben Walker to the table with the young missy wearing that fancy yellow sequined blouse."

Mr. Walker was somewhat startled with himself that such a young beauty should stir his fancy. He eyed Fifi from the corner of one eye and noticed she was sitting bolt upright on Tiny Tim's knee, watching Ben closely. He whistled, tipped his hat, and then blew Meredith a kiss. He chuckled and sniggered at this frivolous yet energetic liveliness.

Suddenly, Alaska Red bolted upright from his seat, stretched his legs, then leaped over to the table where the young girl sat drinking her big Ben Walker. He leaned over the fair maiden and stared down her plunging neckline.

"Well, I'll be! You're the prettiest angel on the face of this earth. Why, look at those rosy cheeks and butterfly eyes. I could write ten poems about you."

Alaska Red felt very elated and grinned like a Cheshire cat. He nuzzled his nose and mouth against Meredith's ear and whispered loudly, "How about a ride in my big green Mac, up the coast to Monterrey? Just you and me."

Meredith held out her delicate hand to the rebel rouser and quite inebriated, agreed, nodding her head up and down.

Fifi could take no more. She rang a bell, and soon the manager appeared. After a few words with the owner, Fifi called security to bring order to the bar. A six-foot-four, three-hundred-pound bouncer, wearing a black jumpsuit and white rubber sneakers, suddenly appeared and escorted Alaska Red back to his seat with the other truckers.

Ben raised his right arm above his head, then banged it heavily on the table.

"I like it, I like it! Served you right, you bum." And he laughed uncontrollably for several minutes.

When he had finished laughing, he stared out the window for a brief period and noticed a young girl no more than twenty years completing her work out at the bus stop. She was slim, well-developed with a very muscular figure. Her golden locks was braided and shone in the sunlight, and her series of stretch exercises completely captivated his attention. He became so fixated on the young girl that he failed to notice Fifi quietly approaching him from behind.

She squeezed his hand and began the chat: "My dear Ben, I apologize for not attending to your needs sooner. Thanks for patiently waiting. I'm at your service – hamburger, meat pie, or fish and chips, which will it be?"

Ben sat motionless, staring out the window at the young athlete. She was awesome!

"Ben – Ben, I'm speaking to you." Fifi chided. "Answer me! Why are you just staring out the window? Are you not feeling well today?"

"Fifi, I'm not staring into space. And no, I am not sick. Look at the bus stop to the right. Have you ever seen a woman work out like that? She's amazing! Look at the muscles on those thighs – they're like two small cantaloupes. And those arms – they're all curve and brawn. Now she's keeping time to the music – those earphones are a great invention. Oh! She's turning this way and staring at me! I must wave to her. She jogs up and down the street every two to three days."

Ben waved to her, but the girl continued keeping time to the music, engrossed with her workout. Tiny Tim, overhearing the bandy between Ben and Fifi, rose quietly from his chair and tiptoed over to the window. Suddenly, he raised his hand and waved to the carefree, cheerful, energetic athlete. The young girl noticed the gesture, and immediately, turned her back to him, and continued the jog on the spot.

Ben was annoyed that Tiny Tim was at the window and pouted like a child. Then he burst into uncontrollable guffaws and kicked the trucker in the shin.

"She gave you the cold shoulder, Mr. Smartie. She knows how to put you in your place."

Tiny Tim withdrew from the window somewhat embarrassed by the gesture of the young woman. He was also very annoyed with the kick from Ben and threatened, "Don't do that again, big boy, or I'll let you have it."

Tiny Tim watched the young girl jog and stretch for a short period of time, then slowly made his way back to the table with the other truckers.

He muttered under his breath, "Some cool fish, she is."

Fifi was beside herself now, and livid with the events at hand. Quietly, she moved away from Ben and made her way to the kitchen. After a brief period, she regained her composure and returned to the dining room.

She sauntered over to Ben and raised her voice: "Mr. Walker, if your erratic behavior continues, you can wheel over to the bar and get your own lunch. and if you behave, I'll include a cherry tart and a free coke."

Ben gave Fifi a gentle nod of the head and said he would behave. As soon as she left his table, he stared once again at the athletic girl so full of life and energy. She was nearing the end of her workout, and stretched her right leg above the head, then made her way to the curb. The lights changed green, and she quickly jogged across the street. Ben pressed his nose into the window and tapped the pane with his table fork. He looked at her steadfastly as she ran briskly down the sidewalk. He was curious about her final destination and continued tapping the windowpane.

Finally, feeling frustrated but somewhat elated, he shouted with a boisterous chortle: "Miss, miss. You'll look at me yet, you flat-chested blond. Can't you give me one second of your time? No? Well, I'll make you give me the time. You wait and see!"

Ben moved away from the window and was upset with the events at hand. He turned to the nearby plant divider and gave it a swift kick with his tattered right boot. One of the plants in a heavy stone pot toppled over the side and fell with a loud thump directly on top of Ben's left foot. He screamed and yelled out loud as fresh sanguineous drainage quickly seeped through the cracks of the old boot and dripped onto the floor. Immediately, he shouted for Fifi, frightened and bewildered by the growing pool of blood.

"My foot, my foot – Fifi! Get this pot off my foot. My bones may be broken. Oh … look how I'm bleeding. Quick, Fifi, get me a bandage. I need help now. Help!"

Fifi ran to Ben's table, pushed the stone pot from his foot, pulled the foul-smelling boot off, and applied pressure with a used napkin at the site of injury. A nearby customer offered his large napkin as a pressure dressing to stop the bleeding. When she was finished dressing his wound, she stood in front of him with both hands on her hips and gave him a disgusted look.

"Mr. Ben, enough is enough. You got carried away with that tall, muscular, perfectly curved young lady, and now you have a serious foot injury. Listen to me, big boy. You need medical attention as soon as possible. I'll call the emergency department at Walston Hospital and tell them you are coming. Someone call a taxi right now."

He grabbed Fifi's wrist and pleaded with her. "I have no money for a cab. Could you lend me some money? I'll pay you back double. Everything is going to be okay."

"You've injured that left foot badly. You need to go to the hospital right now! If the cab doesn't come soon, I'll call an ambulance."

He pulled her to his right side and was frantic. "I must go back to Nigglewood Convalescent first, and attend to some unfinished business there. After that, I'll proceed directly to the hospital."

Fifi was annoyed with Ben. She hesitated and did not reply at once. She noticed he was wiping big tears off his cheeks and finally conceded. Slowly, she pulled a twenty-dollar bill from her pocket and handed it to Ben.

"Here, you, poor soul," she spoke with pity. "A generous gift from a loyal customer. Now go to Nigglewood and settle your affairs there. Then please proceed to the hospital. I'm sure your foot is broken. Look, the napkin is beginning to soil with blood again."

The taxi finally arrived, and within minutes, the injured man was transported back to Nigglewood Convalescent Manor. On his arrival, the secretary at the front desk, seeing his severely injured foot and dressing soaked with blood, rang a bell for assistance and screamed out loud for help. Within seconds, two muscular orderlies appeared and lifted Ben into a private waiting area and undressed him. He cried out in agony as the two assistants redressed the huge, gaping wound on his left foot.

"Mr. Walker, you've lost a lot of blood, and your foot is like ice. I can hardly feel your left foot pulse. Oh! The blood is beginning to stain the new dressing. Help! Help! Someone call an ambulance. We have an emergency here," shrieked one of the assistants.

Ben's head rolled around, and the room began to spin. In a feeble voice, he called out, "Help me, help me. I'm dizzy, and I'm going to faint. Take me to the hospital."

Slowly, he pulled the twenty-dollar bill from his pocket and waved it in front of the orderlies.

"Give this twenty-dollar bill to the taxi driver and thank him for his service. Call a doctor! Now! I need an ambulance …"

Chapter 3
Walston Hospital

Bang! Bang! Ben was jarred awake from his dreamy state of well-being and lightheadedness due to the morphine, and his stretcher, manned by an attendant and an emergency nurse, rolled into the intensive care at two o'clock in the morning. As usual, it was a very busy night, and nurses scurried to and from attending their patients. The stretcher made a squeaky sound as the attendant maneuvered it past the main desk and down the hallway to room 2220. They paused to allow another stretcher carrying a well-filled white plastic bag pass by. Ben craned his neck for a look and was puzzled. What was in the bag? Then he heard an orderly speak to a security officer in a manner filled with jest.

"Welcome to the graveyard shift, Mr. Policeman. This is one dude you won't have to handcuff. Duty calls us to dispatch the dead to the morgue, even at two o'clock in the morning. If the number of dead continue to rise, we'll have to stack them one on top of the other."

The security officer laughed, but was in no mood for talking or jesting, and motioned the orderly on. Ben shuddered and pulled his blue gown over his eyes as the dead body rolled past him. As soon as the corpse disappeared around the corner, he uncovered his head. A stale odor of putrefaction now hung in the air, and he became nauseated with the smell. He began to shiver and asked for an extra blanket. The attendant obtained a warm blanket then bundled him up like a cocoon.

Ben felt lonely and dejected at this early morning hour and longed for his old room at Nigglewood Convalescent. The stretcher rolled into room 2220, and a tall, slender nurse of five feet eight inches with sapphire eyes, blond hair done in pigtails, and muscular arms and legs greeted him at the bedside. She was well-tanned from the summer and wore a deep-blue nursing uniform with an applique of a dove on the chest pocket.

"Hello, Mr. Walker, I'm Gretta Wollenzieder. I will be taking care of you tonight. You look very uncomfortable on that stretcher, so let's transfer you to this special bed for patients at high risk for skin ulcers."

It took a short while for Ben to settle in the new bed and to adjust to the bright overhead lights. But when his eyes accommodated, he realized he had been crying. The nurse appeared as a blur in front of him. Ben rubbed both eyes vigorously with his cold right hand until his vision cleared. Raising his head, he glanced around the room, then focused on the nurse before him. A wave of shock seized him, and he fell into the pillow with a thud. In front of him was the athletic girl he so admired from the window of BacNauld's Bar and Grill!

Speech vanished from his lips for several minutes, and he stared at the beautiful nurse. How he longed to touch her smooth bronze skin, feel her muscular arms, and pass his fingers through her silky golden locks!

Propping himself up on the good elbow, he leaned forward and spoke directly to her: "Miss Gretta, I feel I know you. Why, I often see you working out on Twenty-Sixth street. You are in such great shape, and I envy you."

She smiled graciously. How often had she heard that comment before! Besides, all her patients admired her. She recalled her days as a young girl when she had high hopes of becoming a model. Her parents backed her a hundred percent and secured many modeling opportunities to advance her career. At twelve years of age, she had her first runway show with Toshi of Paris. Despite her success, she felt drawn to a career to help people and decided to become a nurse. She graduated at the top of her class and now had excelled in becoming a very experienced intensive-care nurse. She loved nursing and wanted to make a difference in the field of health.

Glancing at Ben, she recalled seeing him in his wheelchair numerous times but decided to play dumb.

"I don't remember seeing you. I must have a look-alike. Now settle down and let me take your temperature."

Ben knew she was the brawny girl he frequently saw on the streets and became more insistent.

"There is no question in my mind, Gretta. It's definitely you. You always wear your beautiful blond hair in pigtails, a bun, or ringlets, and you sport the most colorful jumpsuits."

"We'll talk about this another time, Ben. Right now, I need you to settle and get some rest. I do have a few questions to ask you before I turn out the lights. Are you having pain in your left foot?"

He nodded and grimaced with pain. Quickly, Gretta got some pain medication, administered it, and took his remaining vital signs. His temperature was ninety-nine degrees Fahrenheit now, and she updated Ben with his progress. Then she did a quick head-to-toe assessment and perused the injured foot. She shriveled her nose at the foul odor.

"That's a nasty-looking left foot, Ben. Here, hold your left thigh with your good hand while I put several pillows under it. It needs to be elevated to bring down the swelling."

Ben looked at her with a cold, icy glare in his eyes. "If only she knew that I'm here because of her," he quietly muttered to himself.

The morphine was taking effect, and Ben relaxed in the pillows and closed his eyes. Ah! The athletic girl he so admired was before him and was his nurse. His thoughts were elated but ambivalent toward Gretta. His mind drifted back to BacNauld's Bar and Grill, and a small rage smoldered in his heart.

His temper flared, and he quietly sputtered out loud: "It's because of her I'm here in this bed – in this awful place – at this lonely hour! I should drop a potted plant on her foot. Then she wouldn't be lifting her leg in the sky or crossing them like a Buddha. Would serve her right!"

Gretta stood motionless at the bedside, observing his behavior.

She whispered to an orderly standing nearby, "What's he saying? Something about a potted plant. I think he's delirious."

The orderly shrugged his shoulders.

"Maybe he's too sensitive to the morphine. His injury certainly doesn't help matters. Let's hope he doesn't get aggressive. Perish the thought if we must restrain him."

Gretta rolled her eyes upward and shivered.

"Let's leave him rest awhile. I'll redress his foot in the morning."

The patient awoke several hours later, and through half-opened eyes, he could see Gretta quietly walking around the bed, writing down vital signs and observing his behavior. A phlebotomist entered the room just then and drew his morning labs. Quickly, Gretta decided to change his foot dressing while he was awake. The foot was tender, reddened, very hot to touch, and was twice the size of his right foot. The odor was putrid now. As soon as she was finished, she elevated the foot once again on several pillows. Within no time, he went back to sleep.

Gretta paused momentarily to look at Ben. Pity surged inside her as she recalled seeing him many times in the wheelchair, rolling down the sidewalk, and calling to her. She had given him a cold shoulder with each encounter and felt guilty for being so callous. She took his right hand and held it for a brief period. Ben opened his eyes, leaned forward, and tried to kiss her forearm, but he fell to one side, too weak to support himself.

"That won't be necessary, Ben. But I have a confession to make. I have seen you many times on the sidewalk and should have stopped to ask if you needed anything. I guess I'm downright selfish, and too absorbed with my workout. I apologize for being so unfriendly."

Gretta felt ashamed and fixed her gaze on a faded wall painting as tears came to her eyes.

Ben patted her soft, muscular hand and spoke, mollified: "Next time, just stop and talk to me. That will drive away the loneliness. There are a lot of things we can talk about."

"I will. I will," she replied emphatically. "Please excuse me for a moment. The phone is ringing, and I need to answer it. I'll be back to do my last check shortly, and we'll talk again. Agreed?"

He nodded his head then lay back on the pillow and dozed off.

Time passed quickly, and soon night gave way to daytime. Sharp at eight-thirty, an attendant entered the room with a breakfast tray and propped Ben up so he could eat. The patient peeked under the tray cover, and his eyes danced with excitement.

"Wow," he blurted out. "There's enough food here for several patients – four slices of bacon, three sausages, porridge, pancakes, scrambled eggs, buttered toast, orange juice, and coffee. I haven't had such a meal in weeks. What's your name, sir?"

"My name is Ricardo Gomez. I help pass the meal trays, give baths, fill the water jugs, and do small errands for the nurses."

"Ricardo, thank you for placing the tray in front of me. No one provides such service at the convalescent home where I live. The food is terrible there, and the used trays sit in the hallway for days. The place is disgusting to live in, yet I have no choice. There's nowhere else to go."

"What place is this, Mr. Walker?"

"Nigglewood Convalescent Manor, my good man," Ben said, irritated.

Ricardo's face went sad, and he pitied Ben. He bowed his head in prayer for him and the facility. May heaven help them!

Finally, Ricardo spoke up, "Sir, you better eat your breakfast before it gets cold. Gretta sends her regards to you. She's gone home now. You were sound asleep when she did her last check, and she didn't want to wake you. I hope the day goes well for you; use the call light if you need me."

"Thanks, Ricardo, I'll be seeing you again, perhaps during the bath?" he asked archly.

"A nurse and I will be helping you. Now I must be finishing handing out the trays. We'll talk again."

As soon as Ricardo exited the room, Ben wolfed down the entire breakfast, and drank a carafe of water in one giant gulp. When his hunger subsided and some of his energy returned, he decided to read a small travel magazine lying on the bedside table. As he perused the exotic destinations, he began to dream of far-flung places, white, sandy beaches, and sparkling turquoise waters.

He whispered softly to himself, "It's good to be alive. I haven't thought of these places in years. To think I once wined and dined in some of those delightful spots."

An eerie silence tiptoed across the room now, and for a moment, all was quiet. Ben was restless in the bed, and this caused throbbing of his infected foot. Memory of his injury at BacNauld's Bar flashed through his mind, and he became increasingly frustrated. He began to pull at his intravenous tubing with quick, sudden jerks. Within minutes, the tubing was ripped apart, and blood began to drip onto the white sheets and the floor.

"There!" he exclaimed. "They're not keeping me here. I'm going back to Nigglewood Convalescent. They won't entangle me in this plastic tubing; nor will they keep me caged in these side rails like a grizzly bear. This is all Gretta's fault."

The distraught patient twisted his body around and pressed his right hand against the bed until the bleeding stopped. His bed had a large stain of fresh blood now. He slid the top of the overhead table back and reached for a package of wet towels in a small server. A spotless mirror popped up from behind the server, and he gave a loud shriek.

"Do I look that bad? Why, I have a beard now, and my hands – they're full of blood. I feel I've aged twenty years since last night. My youth, my vitality, where have they gone? My eyes are sunken, black hollows, and my cheeks hang like gunnysacks. Even my lips are huge. Oh, youth! Where is my blessed youth?"

The reflection of Ben quivered in the mirror, and a throaty, bulldog voice was heard from within.

"Ben," the voice spoke slowly. "You're a mess, and Gretta has fastened you to this bed with a ball and chain. Look at your left foot. You can't go anywhere until that has healed. Our young athlete has you by the noose."

Ben hit the mirror forcefully with his right fist.

"No! No!" he shouted. "She won't hold me in this ridiculous bed. I'll get even with her yet. And you who are you?" he remarked with a sharp, penetrating look. "You shadowed me in the mirror at Nigglewood. What do you want?"

The reflection of Ben wiggled in the mirror. Although he resembled Mr. Walker, he was not human. Neither was he divine. He snapped his fingers, and within seconds, he changed into a demon! On his head, the demon wore a red conical hat tied around the chin, had dark-red fluffy hair to his shoulders, and had a large bluish-purple nose. He was pleasingly plump with russet cheeks, a full face, and peaked bushy brown eyebrows that twitched from time to time. The tops of his ears were sharp points, and the grin was devilish. He twirled round and round, showing off the white and blue gown with sparkles throughout the skirt. In his right hand, he held a mirror. Suddenly, the devil raised one arm and quickly smacked Ben's paralyzed arm.

Ben screeched out loud and yelled at him: "Don't do that again, mister. Or I'll put the server away." He raised his right arm and shook his fist at him.

"There, there," said the demon in a cool voice. "Calm down, control yourself. I gave you a smack to let you know I'm real. You can call me Niggy – that's my nickname. I reside at Nigglewood Convalescent Manor, and I haunt the staff and clients with my sinister presence. Sometimes the doors close, other times the chairs move about, and still other times, I play havoc in the mirrors."

Ben sat nonplussed and motionless. There was a hard, cold gleam in Niggy's black, glittering eyes that made him shudder. The devil's presence was frightening. Ben lay quietly, trying to make sense of the demon. Why was he here? What did he want from him?

Niggy sensed Ben's apprehension and finally spoke: "By now, you must be wondering why I am following you. Well, I have a little sport in mind, and it is very sinister, involving you. Consider the following: Suppose you ask out fair, athletic Gretta to lunch at BacNauld's Bar. I'd choose a day when there are many customers, maybe the three truckers, if you're lucky. Sit her near one of those gigantic flowerpots on the planter by the window. As she is eating and socializing, you kick the planter, so the flowerpot falls on her foot. She will scream, yell, and howl in pain. An eye for an eye, a tooth for a tooth. In a nutshell, evil for evil. It's the law of life. It would serve her right for all the havoc and distress she caused you."

"Yes! Yes! That's it, Niggy. That's it. I can see her howling and writhing in pain. The impact of the flowerpot may even break her foot. Niggy, you are fantastic. Thank you so much, but why are you doing this?"

Niggy remained silent for several minutes and bowed his head below the knees. When the demon rose, his eyebrows were twitching, and his eyes had narrowed and were blacker than ever. An even harder expression etched his plump face.

"Ben, I will tell you my intent, eventually. For now, sufficient for the day is the evil thereof. May I suggest something? Please buy a large mirror for that day. Set the mirror near the planter, so I can watch the entire fiasco. I may even video it. Oh! I can't wait until it happens. Smoke may billow from the mirror, and bells and whistles may be heard. Let's sing some songs and be devilish together."

The two laughed heartily and sang silly songs until they both cried. Ben felt a great release of pent-up aggression. He became so engrossed with Niggy he failed to notice an attendant at the bedside.

Finally, the caregiver spoke in a sharp, curt manner: "Ben, be quiet. You're disturbing the other patients. Why, I can hear you down the hallway. Look!"

The attendant shrieked out loud and pointed to the linen soaked with blood.

"Your intravenous is out, and there's a big pool of blood on the linen and a smaller pool on the floor. Why didn't you call? That's very irresponsible of you. Did you pull it out?"

There was a long pause of silence, then Ben nodded his head sheepishly.

"That's enough silliness from you. Let me clean your hands and get new sheets. I'll call a nurse to start the intravenous. You need it for antibiotics and fluids."

"Yes, sir, yes, sir. I'll obey and be good. I apologize for the inconvenience. Let me help you."

As soon as the attendant had cleaned Ben and the intravenous was restarted, he gave the patient a deep frown.

"If this happens again, I'll put mittens on you."

Ben pushed him away with his right hand, and his temples began to pulsate.

"No mittens for me, sir, or I'll send Niggy your way."

"Who?" questioned the caregiver, rather puzzled.

"Niggy, sir. You'll meet him soon enough. So don't threaten me with mittens, or you may find yourself restrained."

Ben glanced askance at the mirror with the hopes of seeing Niggy, but he had vanished and was nowhere in sight. The attendant remained silent. Then he made the sign of the cross, whispering softly to himself, "God, help this poor soul."

As soon as the attendant left the room, Ben called out for Niggy: "Niggy, Niggy, where are you? Come back. We haven't finished our conversation."

Only the sound of birds chirping could be heard as Ben maneuvered the stand-up mirror for any sign of Niggy. Finally, feeling weary and tired, he fell back onto the pillow and dozed off to sleep.

It was several days before Gretta returned to work, and as usual, she was bubbly and cheerful as she entered the unit. She had just worked out before her shift and was filled with robust energy.

As she entered Ben's room, his face lit up, and he immediately remarked, "Gretta, it's good to see you. You've been away for some time. I presume you had days off?"

"You presume correctly," she replied in a tart, to-the-point manner. "We have a lot of work to do today, and I'm going to start by changing your dressing. After, I'll review a dietary plan with you, and later, I'll do some patient teaching on skin and wound care."

Ben shriveled his nose at Gretta. "Let's start with the dressing change. I want to see my wound today, but I don't want any pain while you're changing the dressing. I can't bear any more pain."

"I'll pre-medicate you first, then begin in fifteen minutes."

As customary when changing dressings, Gretta turned on the television as a diversion from the pain. Today, a young pastoral counselor was talking about comfort and healing and was offering a free book of Psalms to all shut-ins and a follow-up visit if they requested.

"Ben, that program may be for you. The counselor just announced a free, complimentary copy of the Psalms to shut-ins and a follow-up visit if requested. Have you ever read the book of Psalms?"

Ben was taken by surprise with the question, and immediately replied rather abruptly, "Of course, I've read the Psalms. I inherited my great-grandfather's Bible, and it's at Nigglewood Convalescent. I'm as Christian as that counselor is, and I love my Lord. I call him Morningstar. I'm a nomad traveling through this barren land to get to the heavens beyond. I also go to church from time to time when my lady friend can pick me up in the car. I don't need any counselor's visit, and I can manage on my own."

Gretta glanced at the overhead table, and her eyes fell on the upright mirror reflecting beams of golden sunlight throughout the room. She looked intently at it and drew closer. There was an unusual reflection today that rather surprised her.

"Why, Ben," she remarked, astonished, "I reckon you have a double. Look at the image in the mirror. He's the identical reflection of you, except he has a sharp, turned-up nose and pointed ears, and he's wearing clothes suitable for a clown. Look – there he is!"

Gretta shivered slightly as she pointed to the silent intruder. Ben raised his head and glanced at the mirror.

"I don't see anyone. But if you say so, it was Niggy. I spoke to him not so long ago. He told me to have a mirror in my hand. If I get lonely or want company, all I need to do is look into the mirror and within seconds, he promises to appear, what a great place to live! Niggie can dwell in any part of the world."

"Sounds very strange to me." Gretta chided, somewhat indifferent. "Who wants to speak to a phantom? Maybe Niggy, as you call him, is a ghost or a spook. He looks very sinister. Look, I'm shaking at the mere mention of his name."

"Don't be silly. Niggy is a reflection contained in a mirror and is harmless. He won't bite you."

"Ben, I'm changing the subject now. I'm obliged to discuss nutrition with you before discharge. Your appetite is great here, but what will happen when you return to Nigglewood? You told me the meals are terrible there. How about Blueberry Meal Service? The meals are nutritious, and you can have meal service three times a day. It would be much better than BacNauld's Bar and Grill."

"No, it wouldn't be better than BacNauld's Bar and Grill," Ben exclaimed vociferously. "I like the grill because it gives me a chance to get out of Nigglewood. The hamburgers and salads are delicious. Also, my girlfriend Fifi works there. I'd like to invite you to lunch when I've recovered. You can break from your jogging and have a cheese sandwich and a milkshake someday."

Anxious not to offend, Gretta agreed. Then Ben grunted with a small laugh.

"I'm going to be moving to a step-down unit tomorrow. You'll visit me there, won't you, Gretta?"

"Of course. If all goes well, your discharge will be in a week's time. I'll be keeping an eye out for you when I jog. Consider the Blueberry Meal Service. You need the nutrition. I must go now. I have another patient to see. Your foot looks better – the antibiotics are working. Call if you need some pain medication or help. I'll discuss wound care this afternoon."

As soon as she left the room, Ben grabbed the large mirror in the overhead server and maneuvered it again. He peered into it and scrutinized every corner for some sign of the demon. Finally, he spotted him in the far-right hand corner.

"There you are you little rascal. She fell for the idea. I'll keep you informed of my malicious intent. Thank you for restoring my confidence. Your plan is devilish and ingenious. She's totally ignorant of our sinister plot to harm her. This is the best Christmas gift you could give me. All my anger, revenge, suffering, and pain will change to glee, laughter, and celebration with a dash of spite. It feels so good, Niggy. Early Merry Christmas."

"I don't believe in the festive season of Christmas, you bum. However, I do relish in the commercialism and blasé attitude that prevails among many of the shoppers. They cannot get enough of buying. I love to stir these people and wreak havoc among them. I must go now." Niggy hissed in a high-pitched voice.

He passed through the overhead server and proceeded through the room to a nearby window. When he reached the windowsill, he half-turned toward Ben one last time.

"Remember to buy a nice sized mirror and keep it nearby. Your mirror will be capable of reflecting a very bright light or giving a buzzing sound from the handle. Take heed when that happens – I'm nearby. Evil tidings, my friend! Adios."

With that, the demon passed through the window and vanished into the daylight. Ben was awestruck that Niggy could appear and disappear as he pleased. He snuggled into the pillow and closed his eyes. But sleep evaded him. His mind swirled now with thoughts of Gretta and Niggy and every emotion imaginable. He became more and more consumed with the plot developing for BacNauld's Bar and Grill.

"At last," he muttered with bittersweet glee. "At last, there will be some justice."

Chapter 4
To the Streets

Gretta jogged nimbly down Yarma Street to the red traffic light and kept pace on the spot until it turned green. She swayed both hips from side to side, and her muscular form was buoyant with both feet light. She was young, healthy, and a paragon of fitness. Today, she was especially happy about a lunch date at the grill with Ben. She was eager to meet with him and was curious about his health.

No sooner had the light turned green than Gretta was away once again with a skip and a leap. Thanksgiving had passed, and the advent of Christmas had just begun in the city. Excitement and festivity filled the air. The thought of numerous celebrations thrilled her, and occasionally, she danced along the sidewalk. She jogged through several business sections preparing for Christmas until at last she arrived at the grill.

A twinge of excitement and trepidation passed through her as she entered the restaurant and immediately, she asked for Fifi as Ben had instructed her to do. A barman dressed in a white shirt with lace trimming, tight black leather pants, and a green beanie hat motioned for Fifi, who was serving a customer. Shortly, she approached Gretta, eyeing her suspiciously.

"May I help you," she piped up curtly with a faint smile.

Ben had briefed the waitress that Gretta would be coming today, and Fifi was on guard. Gretta sensed the tension in her and went directly to the point.

"I'm here to meet and dine with Ben Walker, a regular customer of yours. He should be here now. It's eleven-thirty, the time he said he would meet me."

"Well, he's not here," Fifi spoke up sharply. "I haven't seen him for three days. Perhaps, you've got your days mixed up, missy."

"No, this is the correct day and time. Ben said he would be sitting at the window near the flower planter. However, I don't see him there."

Fifi raised her eyebrows and glanced at the planter. She felt something was in the air today but couldn't put her finger on it. She paused momentarily and gazed at the gorgeous woman before her. Gretta looked stunning in a red woolen jumpsuit and a black beret hat. The waitress glanced down at her own large bosom, waist-line, and plump thighs, and felt conspicuous.

Feeling irritated, she snapped at Gretta: "I can't help you, young lady. Now I must go back to work."

Then she turned her back and quickly walked away. The bartender whistled under his breath and continued washing beer mugs, all the while watching Gretta askance.

At last, he spoke: "Don't mind her. Fifi is often like that. I must say I haven't seen Ben either. We always have a pint of beer together when he is here and crack a few jokes. He's also one to eye the ladies, and you're no exception. You're very beautiful, young and full of life. Why don't you sit at the bar and have a beer until he arrives? Sometimes he stops at a coffee shop and has a cappuccino coffee with a delicious bagel."

The bartender was smooth, and assertive, and pleased with his advance on Gretta. He poured a draft of Blue Mist, a popular beer, and drew close to her, setting the beer down before her. Conscious of his flirtation, Gretta immediately moved backward toward the door.

"Oh, thank you so much, but I can't have the drink because I am working tonight. Which bagel restaurant is it? I'll try to track him down. I'm disappointed he is not here."

The bartender raised his eyebrows and gazed at Gretta.

"My, she looks stunning today," he mused to himself.

"The dive is called Bagel Jetty and is known to have a rough clientele at times. When you locate him, give him a big hello from me."

Then he grabbed Gretta's hand and squeezed it tightly.

"My name is John Pepper – Pep for short. And yours?"

"I'm Gretta. Nice to meet you, John. Now I must be on my way."

As soon as she was on the sidewalk, she jogged north until the eatery Bagel Jetty appeared. She had butterflies in her stomach and ran up the steps with nervous excitement. It was a busy noontime, and the Jetty was completely full of customers. Waitresses, dressed in blue and white, ran from customer to customer, trying to keep up with the ebb and flow of work. Gretta perused the entire eatery and at last spotted the forlorn-looking man in a far corner.

Quickly, she made her way to Ben but stopped about a foot from him. He had just voided into his pants, and the smell of urine was very pungent and foul. The pants were also covered with dirt and grass, and his gray jacket had buttons missing in the front. A faded green hat lay sideways on his head. Occasionally, he mumbled at customers passing by, but his words were too incomprehensible to understand.

Suddenly, a security officer appeared and made his way to Ben. He was about three hundred pounds, six foot two inches, with salt-and-pepper hair and goatee, and laughing brown-black eyes. A ring of keys jingled from his waist belt, and he held a black baton in one hand.

He knocked the wheelchair with his baton then addressed Ben: "Mr. Walker, it's time to go. The management have asked me to escort you out the door and onto the sidewalk. You've been here two hours dozing in the corner of the restaurant. Come along – you need to be on your way."

The security officer took the wheelchair and rolled it through the congestion of people, out onto the sidewalk.

He pointed the baton at him and remarked, "You need some rest, and that foot needs medical attention. Here is twenty dollars – use it to take a taxi to Walston Hospital."

As soon as the security officer left, Gretta emerged from the shadows and grabbed Ben's arm.

"Ben … Ben … it is you! We were to meet at BacNauld's Bar and Grill today, for lunch. What has happened to you? Why, you've lost so much weight I hardly recognized you. At the time of discharge from Walston Hospital, you had regained your health, and the left foot was healing. I don't believe what I'm seeing! Your foot dressing is very dirty and looks like it has not been changed for some days. This is ridiculous."

An inexpressible sense of angst gripped her as she stared at Ben, and a deep sadness welled up from inside, causing her to waver momentarily. He was very ill! His lifeless form slumped even more to the left, and saliva drooled from both sides of his mouth. A white watery discharge ran constantly from his nose, and he coughed infrequently. His rheumy eyes were inflamed and reddened, and the eye-lids were purplish-blue. Ben had taken to the street, and his wheel-chair was now his permanent dwelling place.

Gretta paused for a moment, fixating her eyes upon Ben before she spoke. Life on the street had its blessings and curses and provided a certain amount of freedom to do things 'their way'. However, for the most part, it was a hard way to live. To provide shelter from the cold, gusty winter winds, Ben had a large green plastic bag draped over the back of the chair and secured to the sides. It fluttered and snapped in the breeze, so much so, that it began to tear on one side. Beneath the faded red, blue, and white American flags tied to the brake was a large, netted bag filled with empty and full bottles of water, used clothes, chocolate bars, dried fruit, and tins of preserved meat. On the other side of the chair, an old radio was secured to the armrest by a small rotating mirror.

Ben glanced furtively at Gretta, then wheeled his chair around to face the street. As he reached for a bottle of water in the netted bag, the motion caused the chair to careen slightly, and the bottles began to drop on to the pavement.

"Ben, Ben, leave the bottles, and I'll pick them up. You need to get away from the curb," Gretta called out.

She ran over to the chair, grabbed the handles, and steadied it. Then she pulled it back away from the curb and turned it around to face her. Ben's hollow, black, sunken eyes gazed upward at her clear blue eyes, and he paused to admire her muscular figure pulsating with life and energy.

Finally, he spoke, his speech thick and slurred: "Gretta, my dear. Thank you for stopping my wheelchair from rolling into the street. Oh, I'm sick, very sick. I'm sorry about our lunch date – I had every intention of being there. But the pain in my left foot is excruciating, and my temperature is at a boiling point. I feel terrible today."

"You are very sick, Ben. You've got that right."

She glanced at Ben's left foot again, and noticed the dressing change date went back to his last day at Walston Hospital. It had not been changed since then. The young nurse held her breath and felt nauseated – the dirty bloodstained dressing exuded a very foul odor. Ben was septic again, and his condition was serious.

Gretta prodded Ben about the dressing. "What happened since your discharge from Walston Hospital? Why wasn't your dressing changed daily as ordered?"

Ben looked at Gretta with a dazed expression in his eyes and was silent for a period of time. He was too sick to socialize today, and he stared at the street packed with cars, trucks, and buses going about. He wanted to slip away into oblivion with them.

Finally, he faced Gretta and spoke: "Yes, my dear nurse, this is the same dressing from Walston Hospital, and it hasn't been changed since my discharge. The visiting nurse came several times to change it, but I was out and about with Cleaver, my buddy, or I was at BacNauld's Bar and Grill. I'm not irresponsible, Gretta. I just detest Nigglewood Convalescent. Since I've returned to the dastard place, my sheets haven't been changed, the food is worse, and the cockroaches are still in my bed. They won't do anything to stop those pests. I had no choice but to take to the streets."

Gretta was aghast by what she heard, and gingerly stepped up to Ben, placed both arms around his shoulders. She drew the dirty, foul-smelling figure to herself as she held him in her arms; she was aware his skin was very warm.

"My, your skin does feel hot. Have you checked your temperature recently?"

He shook his head from side to side. Gretta touched his forehead, and it felt even hotter. The lifeless figure began to shiver in the cool, damp wind, and both knew he was becoming sicker by the moment.

"Ben, you must go to the hospital now. You're very ill, and your foot needs urgent attention. There's a foul odor from the old dressing, and I'm sure it is very infected."

Ben pushed himself away from Gretta and remarked weakly, "I won't go to any hospital. I'll be wheeling to the makeshift shelter at the beach after I have a bite to eat. My two beach bums will be waiting for me. We have our gin or rum to heat us up for the night, a puff or two of marijuana, some leftover hamburgers from the dumpster, and a soda pop or two. Then we snuggle into a corner of the shelter and cover ourselves with dirty, old blankets. As long as the cockroaches are in my bed at Nigglewood, I'm a man of the streets. I'm not going back there, and that's that."

Just then, he leaned over and adjusted his left foot on the foot-rest. A small, weak cry of discomfort was heard, and he held his foot, hoping to ease the pain.

"My foot is so sore, Gretta. So sore. Last night, I took four aspirins and three Tylenols to get to sleep. I cried and cried until finally I dozed off, but it was a restless night. When I woke up in the early morning hours, the pain was there to greet me. I couldn't move my leg for a while."

"You need medical attention, Ben. You have a very bad infection in your foot. Anyone will tell you that. I'll take you to the hospital. And … and …"

Gretta's voice escalated now, and she spoke more rapidly, trying to verbalize her many thoughts.

"I'm going to call the Housing and Apartment Bureau, and report that there are cockroaches at Nigglewood Convalescent. Also, I'm going to mention the bedsheets aren't being changed and the meals are anything but nutritious. We have a right to complain."

He raised his right arm and clumsily pushed her away from the wheelchair.

There was a wild expression on his face now, and he lashed out at Gretta: "Don't bother. It will only make matters worse. And I'm not going to the hospital. It's too depressing, and they can't do anything for me. Leave me alone."

Ben unlocked his brakes and began to move away from the curb into the street.

Gretta was beside herself and shrieked, "The light is red, Ben. Come back onto the sidewalk, or you'll be hit by a vehicle!"

Cars were whizzing by him, so he maneuvered his chair back onto the sidewalk. Gretta breathed a sigh of relief and motioned him to wheel over to where she was standing. Anxious to detain him as long as possible, her mind raced for thoughts.

"Ben, that was close. Don't do that again. Let me take you to a restaurant and buy you lunch. I can look at your foot and redo the dressing while you are having something to eat."

"No, I don't want you touching my foot. I'll get my own food. I don't need your help. Now go away."

Gretta pressed further, "Let's call the Housing and Apartment Bureau and tell them about your situation at Nigglewood Convalescent. The cockroaches should not be in your bed, your room needs a desperate clean, and meals on wheels should be served. You need good nutrition that is consistent."

"No, no, no," cried Ben in defiance. "I'm not going back there. I'm a man of the streets now, and I don't want to be bothered."

Gretta knew she was losing the fight with Ben. She tried one last time: "Do you still go to Maranatha Fellowship? You mentioned at Walston Hospital that you liked the people that attended there."

Ben stared at Gretta with his dark, glassy eyes, and his facial expression changed to one of sadness. Finally, he piped up with disagreeable asperity.

"Yes, I still go to Maranatha Fellowship when I can. My lady friend hasn't been very attentive to me these days, so my attendance has been sadly lacking. I still read my Bible. It's all that I have right now. As to friends in the fellowship – no, I don't need them. I must say, however, they have some mighty pretty ladies. Now I must be on my way to the beach. Don't follow me. I don't need your help. Leave me alone!"

The light turned green just then, and angrily, he swung his chair onto the street and rolled across in a zigzag fashion. Once he reached the other side, he made his way to the beach. From time to time, he glanced backward and could still see Gretta. His left foot was throbbing continuously and sending sharp shafts of pain up into his inner thigh. His unmitigated suffering was almost unbearable. Yet, despite all that, he was able to greet well-wishers along the way. One compassionate pedestrian took a ten-dollar bill out of his pocket and squeezed it in his hand. Ben thanked him and sped on. Soon he became a miniature silhouette in the distance, and then disappeared on the beachfront.

Gretta stood motionless, watching Ben disappear. She wiped big tears from her eyes and pitied him. She was nervous now. Ben's will to live was slowly slipping away, and if he did not receive medical attention shortly, he would not live more than two to three days.

She thought back to his predicament and tried to make sense of it. Medical attention was first and foremost; second, his living quarters at Nigglewood Convalescent needed to be reported. She decided that now was the perfect time to call the housing authorities.

"Yes," she cried out loud. "I'll call the Housing and Apartment Bureau myself and arrange an appointment to speak with someone who can investigate the premises. After that, I'll go and find Ben and bring him to Walston Hospital, one way or another. His childlike rebellion with all his sorrow and suffering will finally stop."

She walked over to a payphone near a small bed and breakfast hotel and called the bureau. The secretary answered in a cordial fashion and informed Gretta all their agents were away for the afternoon. However, she could arrange an appointment with Mr. John Dicton tomorrow morning at ten o' clock. Gretta thanked her, accepted the appointment, and then made her way home.

Next morning, Gretta arrived at the bureau and was ushered into John Dicton's office at exactly ten o' dock. Mr. Dicton had been reading and studying reports since eight o'clock in the morning and was glad for the reprieve from this. Dicton was a middle-aged man wearing black horn-rimmed glasses, a brown tweed jacket, and beige pants. His hair was a mass of dark brown curls with streaks of white, his eyes a kindly blue, and his face handsome. He wore dark-green shoes and a gold bracelet, a gift from an old client. He raised his bushy black eyebrows and spoke with a saturnine smile:

"Good morning, Miss Wollenzieder. How may I help you?" Greta sat up erect and was somewhat uncomfortable in the chair. "You may call me Gretta, Mr. Dicton. I'm here to report a deterioration of care in a facility known as Nigglewood Convalescent Manor. A patient of mine, Mr. Walker, informed me of such poor care that he has taken to the streets as a homeless person and vows never to go back unless they change their practices."

Dicton leaned back in his swivel chair, raised his right green shoe onto this left leg, and rotated a gold pen in his hand. The last place he wanted to investigate was Nigglewood Convalescent Manor. He was well aware of the numerous investigations in the past and would do all to avoid a scrutiny of the facility at present.

Gazing at Gretta, he enquired: "What do you mean by a deterioration in care? We investigated the facility six months ago, and the care met our standards. The only things that needed some repairs were light fixtures, the outlets, and several fire alarms."

Gretta's eyes flashed with indignation, and she fired back: "Ben tells me there are cockroaches in his bed, the sheets aren't changed every week, and the garbage piles higher and higher with no one to pick it up, and the meals are terrible. The staff no longer bring the food tray to him —they leave it outside the room. There are numerous times when he has not eaten because no one is around to help. His room hasn't been cleaned in weeks, and the bathroom odor is disgusting. This is happening to others as well."

Dicton stared at Gretta, and for a moment, quietly admired this plucky lady. She was beautiful, poised, and determined. He paused to reflect on the situation under discussion and was reluctant to proceed with any investigation.

However, he realized Gretta was becoming more aggressive and he piped up: "What do you propose I do? I don't know if arriving on their doorstep today or tomorrow would be profitable."

"Well, Mr. Dicton, I'm also getting a task force together at Walston Hospital, and we are going to visit the facility very shortly. A hospital administrator, a doctor, a dietitian, and several nurses are going to check the rooms and the dietary services. Then we will send our findings and recommendations to you."

Dicton felt squeezed into a corner and had to decide on a plan.

"Okay. Okay," he said curtly, raising his hands above his head. "I'll get on to it right away, and we'll survey the facility either tomorrow or next Monday. I'll contact you when we've completed our visit."

"Thank you so much, Mr. Dicton. I greatly appreciate your efforts. I look forward to hearing from you."

She rose from the chair, shook Mr. Dicton's hand, then left the bureau to find Ben. It was a cold, windy day, and Gretta bundled the red mohair scarf around her neck and shoulders. Several shelters were near the beach walkway, and she decided to visit each one. In the first shelter, men and women were still sleeping and huddled close together because of the wind. She moved on to the next shelter, occupied by men only. A strong odor of wine and marijuana pierced the air and caused Gretta to wretch with nausea. Several men were up and about listening to a radio or performing their morning toilet. She asked one man if he had seen a homeless man named Ben Walker, with a lame left leg and arm riding in a wheelchair. The man said he had seen him two nights ago but not since then. The next shelter was mixed again, but the inhabitants were up and about. Gretta asked a middle-aged woman wearing a dirty purple dress, black boots, and chains of silver if she too had seen Ben. The woman smiled with her dirty black teeth and said no. If she had seen him, she would have offered him a sweet laced with heroin.

Gretta looked at her watch. Three hours on the beach had passed quickly, and it was now two o'clock. There was no sign of Ben anywhere. Her stomach rumbled as a reminder that she hadn't eaten since early morning. She walked quickly back to the main business area and decided to eat a late lunch at BacNauld's Bar and Grill. Trying to locate Ben would be no easy task, and she would resume her search tomorrow. With a determined step, she kicked up her heels and jogged hastily to the grill.

Chapter 5
Dance of Demons

It was a cold, frosty evening, and the large fall moon cast its blue white rays on the ground below, heralding another chilly, freezing night. A slush from the daytime had now hardened, and the walk on the sidewalks was treacherous. Gretta stepped carefully, avoiding the occasional puddles of water. At one point, she stopped to roll up her nursing pants so they wouldn't get dirty from the soft mud on the sidewalk. As she strolled carefully to work, she pondered over the activities of the past few days. Mr. Dicton had informed her his bureau had begun their investigation at Nigglewood Convalescent and would call her when they were finished. She was pleased with his effort.

The thought of Ben and his predicament brought a surge of sadness, and she was very upset he had not been located. She decided to look for him one last time in the coming week, and if that failed, she would go to the police and file a missing person's report. She would let the police take over for her. Thoughts of finding Ben dead crossed her mind, and tears came to her eyes. Walston Hospital Emergency Department appeared now, and Gretta breathed a sigh of relief.

As soon as she was in the hospital, she made her way to the intensive care. As she stepped off the elevator, various coworkers who had just finished their shift saluted her on their way home. A whirl of excitement caught her, and she was pleased to be at work. Her spirits became elated when she saw numerous Christmas decorations in the hallway and in the patients' rooms. Christmas cards and pictures of former staff and their families were pinned to a large bulletin board. Traditional carol music played softly in the background, and several nursing attendants decorated a lush green fir tree. Near the computer station was a small wooden table filled with boxes of chocolates, and tins of popcorn, peanut brittle and fruitcake. Several bottles of apple cider and containers of eggnog were in one corner. All this was a token from appreciative family members.

Gretta stood motionless, admiring the decorations and sighed with joy.

"Ah, this is a great time to be alive."

A nursing team leader sitting at the monitor desk looked up anxiously when she saw Gretta and greeted her cordially but with a sullen facial expression.

"It's good to see you, Gretta. I hope you had a good rest and are ready for work. It's very busy tonight."

"Thank you, Carol. I've had a good rest, and I'm always ready for work. What is my patient assignment tonight?"

"I've given you a very challenging assignment because you are the most experienced nurse this shift. Mr. Ben Walker, a former patient of ours, was readmitted yesterday afternoon. He is very ill, and I doubt whether he will make the night. They are coding him right now for the third time."

Gretta's face went white, and she was assailed by a sick qualm for several moments. She struggled to find words to convey her dismay and finally spoke as she held onto a corner of the nursing station: "Carol, I know the patient all too well. I saw him on the street several days ago, and I knew he was very sick then. His left foot was swollen, and he was in a lot of pain. I tried to encourage him to go to Walston Hospital, but he refused and went to the beach instead."

Carol was uneasy but spoke imperturbably, "You have a lot of support staff with you tonight. I'll be there shortly to help."

Gretta's stomach churned, and she groaned with indigestion, but she made her way quickly to room 3633. She felt weak and anxious as she stepped into the room. A quick glance at Ben sent shock waves spiraling up her spinal cord. Intravenous drips, each with a particular medication, surrounded him on both sides. A respiratory ventilator quietly hummed in one corner; a red light flashed on and off, alerting the staff to the need for suctioning. A continuous dialysis machine clicked away as fluid moved in and out of a right groin access. On top of Ben was a green cooling blanket for a temperature of 103 degrees Fahrenheit. Ben's size had doubled in the last few days, and he now occupied the whole bed. His abdomen protruded into the air like a large balloon, and his eyes, face, and extremities were grossly edematous. Foot splints, too small to support his giant legs, lay on one side of the bed. At the head of the bed was Dr. French, directing the code blue, and nursing staff and interns were around each side.

Dr. French glanced at the monitor and shouted out loud, "We're in torsades de pointes. Get a magnesium drip up and prepare to shock. Another dose of epinephrine, please. How long have we been running the code?"

The day nurse looked at the code sheet and announced briskly, "Twenty five minutes, Dr. French."

"One more round of drugs plus shocking. If this doesn't alter his course of therapy, I'll call the code."

Shortly, the code was called by Dr. French, and Ben was dead. Gretta was petrified by the events before her and stared at Ben. Her mind went blank, and her heart fluttered. She was in complete shock. She backed away from all the commotion, excused herself from the room, and sat down in a chair in the hallway. She lowered her head between both legs for a short period, tears flowing from her eyes. Ben's day nurse saw her slumped over in the chair and came to comfort her.

"It's okay, Gretta. It's okay to cry."

And she put her arms around the slouched figure and hugged her. On the other side of the wall, in room 3633, the atmosphere had changed and had become very much alive. Although Ben was clinically dead, his spirit was animated with life; and he rose from the bed and dangled his legs over the side. He pulled the invasive lines out and stood at the end of the bed, looking around the room. No one was in the room now, and silence permeated every corner. He felt light, free, easy, and had no pain. No pain! He took a few steps and realized he could walk. His feet and the bones of his ankles were made strong again, and he leaped for joy around the room.

He wandered over to the mirror in the bathroom and gave a small shriek. His look was terrible, and his physical appearance was still grotesque. Hair had grown beyond his neck in the last few days and was now a dull-gray color. The eye sockets were still sunken, and his eyes were dark grayish-black and suffused with blood. His complexion was a reddish-blue, and tape marks from the endotracheal tube streaked the sides of his puffy cheeks. His abdomen remained very distended, and the soiled gown barely covered him. Although his appearance was sadly lacking, yet he was filled with joy, and his eyes exuded warmth, liveliness, and peace.

As he continued to stare in the mirror, he noticed a small devilish person in one corner. It was Niggy. Soon, Niggy occupied the entire mirror and appeared very distraught and vexed. Ben was now in the Spirit without any discomfort.

"Beastly! Beastly! You are a most heedless and absurd man. You are no longer human, controlled by lust, you rascal. You are flesh controlled by the Spirit. How I loathe you! How did that come about?"

Ben looked at Niggy with his warm, kindly eyes. No longer did he have to fight or prove his point. He was above that now. He moved closer to the mirror to touch Niggy.

"I'm sorry you're so distraught with me. I no longer feel alone or deserted in this world. I feel loved and want to love back. That's the name of the game."

Tears came to Niggy's somber eyes, and they flashed with indignation. He turned away from Ben for a moment to dry them and to collect his thoughts. Then with a cold, stern look, he finally took courage and faced Ben.

"You idiot! I'll show you a thing or two."

Niggy pulled out a white glistening baton from his waist and waved it at him.

"Do you see this? When I wave it, myriads of devils and the Grand Devil will be in your room. Watch! Here they come!"

Niggy waved the baton in the air, and immediately, the room began to fill with gray smoke. Within minutes, midget-sized demons passed through the walls without a sound and made their way to Ben. All totaled, there were approximately two hundred miniature demons dressed in bright satin colors of blue, yellow or red. Each demon wore a green dunce cap on his head and a red cape over one shoulder. Around each waist was a huge, buckled belt with tiny bells. When they moved, there was a cacophony of bells ringing.

Each demon held a small pitchfork in one hand and moved about in rhythmic fashion, singing, "Ben, Ben, you're a ten. Come to us and be our friend."

The demons closed in on Ben now, and soon surrounded him. The singing grew louder and louder.

"No, no," shouted Ben. "I can't be one of you. I'm not a demon, and I have no desire to be one. I'm waiting. I'm waiting for someone – an angel or seraphim – someone who will take me to Morningstar. Get away from me, you, you evil ones. Go, get out of here."

The demons pressed in on Ben even further and continued to chant their song. Suddenly, the room began to whirl in clockwise fashion, and bright flashing lights burst forth from the floor and the doorway. A stunning demon dressed in a sparkling black and white jumpsuit with a matching floor-length cape appeared in the room and eyed Ben. He had a lively, sculptured face, brown eyes that were bright and very alive, and had glistening hair of silver and black pulled into a chignon. His cheeks were russet, his look, fiery and penetrating. In one hand, he held a blue magic wand; and in the other, a crystal, stargazing ball that whirled at lightning speed. He raised the magic wand high in the air and out came shooting stars, fireballs, and small iridescent rockets. The two hundred demons bowed to him, then retreated into the background of darkness with only their legs and arms showing. The dazzling figure moved to Ben.

Ben moved away from the devil and exclaimed, "No, no, get away from me. I don't want any part of you. Morningstar? Morningstar, where are you? I need you now. Help me!" Ben shouted out loud.

Ben was unnerved by the Grand Devil and stared sideways at the arms and legs of the miniature devils. The Grand Devil shook his head disapprovingly, and with a face full of mockery, stood in front of him and finally spoke: "I am the Grand Devil, who has come to take you to the infernal kingdom. I am not going to hurt you. On the contrary, I am here to help you evolve to a new level of being in Devil Land. There you will be welcomed like a prince, meet King Lucifer, and start a new life as a devil. You will receive daily massages, visit other devils, go to devil theatre, and perhaps study devil ballet or modern dance. There are also rides at Pitchfork Sports Land, magicians wielding great power in black magic, and jumps from The Flaming Horse Riders. Come, Ben. It's a chance of a lifetime."

"No, get away from me – please."

Tears filled his eyes, and he gazed at the Grand Devil with pity. Finally, he could no longer contain himself, and he wept quietly.

When he had finished crying, he spoke: "I want to love my enemies, love those who hate me, love my brothers and sisters, and love Morningstar who redeemed me. This is my goal now."

"Enough, enough," the Grand Devil cried, stomping his feet.

He waved the wand across his chest, and immediately, everything went completely black. Thunder and lightning spewed forth from the wand, and balls of fire and shooting stars flew everywhere. Multicolored lights flashed on and off, and the little demons could be heard talking loudly about ways to break Ben's will. Suddenly, equipment started to move about in the room, and furniture began to shake. The little demons started to screech and howl and run about in a haphazard fashion until several figures were knocked onto their backs. They cried out loud in agony until other devils pulled them up by their hair. There was a mad stampede for the doorway by the two hundred devils just then as they tried to exit from the room. The Grand Devil, now enshrouded in black, laughed hysterically as he watched the tiny culprits squeeze and push past the doorframe. Then he raised the wand above his head, waved it in the air, and vanished from sight.

Following the Grand Devil's departure, a huge grayish-white cloud of smoke hung in the air. The little devils continued to squeeze and shove one another out of the room until finally the door closed with a loud bang. Soft groans could be heard outside the room, and occasionally, the sharp scratching of fingernails on the room window.

However, one small demon remained behind, hidden in a dark corner, observing everything that transpired. It was Niggy.

Soon a cool breeze could be felt blustering through the room, and very shortly, it began to blow on Ben. Then sounds of horses moving rapidly and wildly pierced the air, and Ben turned in the direction of the noise. He saw thousands of glistening white stallions with angels on them. Each angel carried a shield in one hand and a sword in the other and was prepared for battle. On their backs were bows and arrows, and on their heads were bright-red helmets. The angels were dressed in snow-white garments that covered the knees. In front was the lead captain of the entire army, archangel Haviara, driving a white-and-gold chariot. He cracked a gold whip, and his six magnificent white steeds galloped at breakneck speed to earth. Archangel Haviara entered the room and disembarked from the chariot. He spoke to the myriad of angels on horses to be silent, and soon all was quiet.

Ben was stunned by the heavenly host of angels in front of him, went down on his knees, and fell prostrate before them. They were given to orderliness and sat obliquely on their horses, one after another. Their shields were before them, with swords in position to strike. About five hundred angels had bows and arrows drawn, ready for action.

Ben cleared his throat, turned to the captain, and asked, somewhat bewildered, "Are you with me or with them?"

"Neither," said the captain graciously. "I am archangel Haviara of the Celestial Heavens and captain of all the angels in Morningstar's army. Now I have come for you."

And Ben fell on his face to the floor in reverence and said, "What does Morningstar say to his servant?"

The captain said to him, "Take off your slippers from your feet, for the place where you are standing is holy."

And Ben did so.

Ben was mesmerized by the nine-foot-tall captain before him. He wore a glistening white-and-gold tunic that covered the right shoulder and draped both knees. The other shoulder was bare, muscular, and fully developed. His diamond-covered gray helmet completely covered his head, and his ivory-colored hair fell beneath to the shoulders. His azure eyes were soft and kindly. In his right hand was a flaming, golden sword, one almost as tall as he, which rotated in all directions. He stepped forward and spoke in a melodious voice with a faint but recognizable heavenly lilt:

"Don't be afraid, Ben. I've come to take you to Morningstar. Are you ready?"

For a moment, Ben froze with fear; but shortly, he felt tender feelings pass through him, and he replied with good-natured affection, "I haven't had time to clean up and make myself presentable for Morningstar."

The captain touched his arm and spoke in a voice, as clear as a ringing bell: "Come as you are, Ben. We must leave now, or the Grand Devil and the demons will come back to stage a fight for you. Get into the chariot."

Slowly, Ben made his way to the chariot with the captain and with joyful eagerness sat in the chair next to him. Then the captain cracked his whip, and the beautiful white stallions neighed, went up on their hind feet, and rose in the air. Soon Ben was out of sight.

Niggy came out of the dark corner and stared as Ben, the Captain, and the thousands of angels disappeared into the night. When they finally vanished, he stomped about with rage and sounded a barrage of swear words.

When he calmed down, he soliloquized to himself: "Darn it, they got away. How am I to make sense of all of this? If a battle had been called against the heavenly hosts, it would have been disastrous. Their light is so overpowering we devils would be blinded. That's disgusting! Ben's corpse lies on the bed, but he is now flesh – controlled by the Spirit. I'd give anything to see Celestial

Heavens where he has gone. Ah! He still has a friend Gretta outside the room. Perhaps, I can convince her to go to this paradise of God with me. Watch me."

Outside the room, Gretta had finished crying and was drying her saddened blue eyes on some tissue.

She spoke mournfully to the support nurse beside her: "I think I've cried my heart out for Ben. Give me ten minutes alone with him. Then I'll be ready to pack the body with you and tidy the room."

"Ten minutes, Gretta. That's it! Already there's a patient in emergency assigned to this bed, and they're anxious to move him as soon as possible."

Gretta entered the room and stared at the lifeless figure in front of her. She started to cry again and made her way to the corpse. The odor of death and putrefaction could be smelt everywhere, and she felt queasy again. Once she was at the bedside, she put her arms around his protruding abdomen and wept uncontrollably. She was no more than five minutes at the bedside when she felt a sharp prick in her right kneecap. She glanced around the room until her eyes fell on a little devil standing beside her, holding a small pitchfork.

"Who are you?" she shouted angrily at him.

"I'm Niggy, a demon from Devil Land. I roam the earth seeking whom I can devour. I tried to prevent Ben from going to Celestial Heavens to meet Morningstar. Alas, I failed. Now I am making plans to go to Celestial Heavens, myself. Perhaps, you would care to join me? What do you have to say for yourself, Miss Perfect, Sustainer of Life?"

Gretta was very annoyed with Niggy and spoke abruptly to him, her lips quivering with every word: "What is this about Celestial Heavens and Morningstar? Ben is deceased. How do you know he is meeting Morningstar?"

Niggy felt a small sense of security and did a whirling dance on the spot. Then he wiggled the bells on his feet, flared his red cape, and waved his pitchfork in the air. Butterflies and bees came out of the fork and flew around the room.

After a few moments of this reverie, he stopped and spoke up in a shrill, menacing voice: "Mr. Ben left about fifteen minutes ago, earth time, for Celestial Heavens with the captain, archangel Haviara, and his host of angels. It was quite a sight. You could hear them for miles before they arrived in the room. The horses' hooves were pounding the heavens in pursuit of earth. When they arrived, the captain told them to remain silent and on standby, in case there were problems from the Grand Devil and the two hundred demons that had just left the room. I'd love to see Celestial Heavens and the great Morningstar, and I'm scheming ways to get there. And you are going to help me."

Niggy burst out laughing but was filled with contempt for the beleaguered nurse.

Gretta spoke up quickly, annoyed with his mockery of her: "Celestial Heavens is a place for saints, angels, those who are dead but will rise again someday, and for those who are living when He comes. You're a devil, and you can't go there. But I will go there when I die. That's the wonderful hope I have after this life."

Niggy sneered at her and jested.

"You're rather assertive, Miss Smartie Pants. You're stubborn and defiant and will not be going to the heavens anytime soon. You have a big hurdle to cross. This disastrous death of Ben Walker is all your fault. Ben was watching you from a restaurant window when a flowerpot fell on his foot. The injury was serious, and eventually, he died from it. If he were alive today, you silly woman, he'd have his revenge. The flowerpot would be falling on your foot. 'Good riddance,' he would say. You caused all his pain and suffering. Shame on you! Now, if you want, you can get down on your knees and confess your transgressions to me. Under the law of devils, I will pardon you."

Gretta's face flushed crimson.

"I don't believe one word of what you are saying. And I will not bow to you or ask for a pardon from you. You are ridiculous. Get away from me and leave the room. Now!"

"No, I will not! I'm just getting started with you. You're going to join me and become a devil. I'm going to see to it."

Niggy pulled back his cape and withdrew a gold and green-jeweled sabre. He moved slowly toward Gretta and taunted her.

"Are you ready to come with me, dear Gretta?"

"No, I am not," exclaimed Gretta in a state of frenzy. "Get away from me. Help, help, someone – I'm being attacked by a devil."

Gretta moved away, but Niggy cornered her between the bed and the wall.

A warm breeze began to blow in the room just then, and papers, equipment, intravenous poles, and the medication server began to move about. Bright lights blinked on and off as a thick cloud of blue smoke moved across the room and stopped short of the doorway and hovered there. A glistening shadow stood in the doorway now, and soon Gretta discovered it was a dove. The dove was stunningly beautiful and held the attention of both nurse and devil.

The dove waddled over to Gretta, cooed gently, then ruffled its feathers. The bird was six feet tall, completely white with silver-blue etching on the tips of its wings. Its eyes shone like two brilliant emeralds, and its feet were covered in diamond dust. It sparkled continuously as it moved about on the spot.

Finally, it spoke: "Gretta, I'm White Dove, a special dove from Celestial Heavens. I've been sent by Morningstar to pick you up and take you to the Heavens. I understand from the Prince of Peace that you still have some unfinished business with Ben Walker. You wanted him to call the Housing Bureau with you and possibly to see Mr. Dicton? Now is the time to make the amends."

Gretta's excited and friendly eyes sparkled in the dove's presence, and she spoke up: "I'm so glad you've arrived, White Dove. I was disappointed with Ben that he did not join me in the interview with Mr. Dicton, and I would like to discuss it with him. It still annoys me that I could not find him on the beach. Now I have another problem. This awful demon, Niggy, says I'm to blame for Ben's injured foot and death. Nothing could be further from the truth." She began to weep softly, all the while eyeing the bird.

The dove looked around the room until it spotted Niggy near one corner of the bed. It stared at the demon with pity and inquired.

"What do you have to say for yourself?"

"I have a lot to say." Niggy piped up. "White Dove, it is true. This woman caused Ben's injured foot, sickness, and death. Ben and I were plotting a scenario whereby the flowerpot would fall on her foot, hopefully breaking it. She would feel the pain and suffering he went through. Now I'm going with you to Celestial Heavens. I want to see Ben and Morningstar. Away, let's get going. Gretta can stay here on earth."

The dove stared at the little demon with curiosity, then cooed.

"You are a devil, Niggy, and can't come. Celestial Heavens is for those who believe. You are evil, Gretta is good. Gretta believes in Morningstar, the Truth. So, away with you."

The dove raised one foot and gave Niggy a small kick that sent him flying across the room.

He hit the wall with a loud thump, then yelled and screeched out loud: "You beast. Truth and Evil are beside the point. I'm going with you to Celestial Heavens."

The dove prodded Gretta to mount one of its wings. Then it pushed her gently to its back, and quietly passed through the walls of Walston Hospital, and disappeared into the dark of night.

Niggy watched as the two vanished and was furious. He stomped his feet on the floor again and clung to his wand and pitchfork.

He mumbled to himself, "Gretta will be back on earth, and I'll corner her another time. Besides, she can give me an update of Celestial Heavens. I'm not finished with her yet. I'll make it to the Heavens soon!"

As soon as the dove passed through the last of the fluffy gray black clouds, he soared into the light of the yellow-orange sun. The sun shone warmly, and its rays went in all directions. Behind it was the vast expanse of azure and lilac skyline. Soon lustrous rolling parklands and woodlands appeared in brilliant green, and one could see sections of dark black soil. Then countless mansions of every color became visible and stretched for miles into the heavens. A delicate fragrance of Chloe and Frankincense permeated the air, and large birds with magnificent flowers in their beaks flew about while colorful butterflies rested on the castle entrance.

At length, the dove came to rest on the doorstep of a sprawling light-pink mansion that stretched two miles long and one mile wide.

In one corner, the castle was dominated by a clock tower. Numerous autographs were scratched into the clock base. The building was decorated with turrets, spires, and domes; a deep wide moat with crystal blue water went around the mansion. A pristine white marble aqueduct crossed the moat, allowing inhabitants and guests to come and go. The dove lowered Gretta onto the white marble aqueduct, then pecked a shiny silver ball near a huge oval door. Chimes sounded from the castle tower, and bells rang up the mountains. Suddenly, the massive door slid open, and the dove and Gretta entered a spacious pink and white foyer with a high-domed ceiling. When the door slid shut, the dove bid her adieu, then vanished through a side wall.

All was quiet now, and Gretta stood motionless, taking in the majestic surroundings. She noticed a small sign on a winding staircase to the left of her that read, 'Welcome to Celestial Heavens.'

Above the sign was a white cord that, when pulled, announced the arrival of visitors. Gretta moved to the white cord and pulled it. The entrance was filled with beautiful strains of music for several minutes. Then two cherubs dressed in red mini gowns appeared at the top of the stairwell. Each cherub had a shiny brass trumpet in one hand. When they sounded the trumpets, archangel Haviara appeared on the staircase. He moved slowly down the stairs until he was near Gretta. Gretta shook with fear and fell flat on the floor.

The archangel asked her to rise and spoke kindly and gently to her: "Greetings, my dear one, and fear not. I am archangel Haviara, Captain of the Lord's armies. Your friend, Ben Walker, is here in the Celestial Heavens and is being groomed to meet Morningstar very soon. There was such a celebration when he arrived in the heavens. Clarions sounded, harps played, and choirs of angels sang. He was very excited with the greeting but was tired from the journey."

Gretta cried big tears of joy at the news. Try as she may, she could not stop crying.

Finally, archangel Haviara spoke again, giving wise counsel: "You are not in the spirit yet, so you must stay here in the foyer of this castle. I'll see how Ben is doing and tell him you've come to visit for a brief period."

Gretta thanked the archangel, then wiped back her tears. Archangel Haviara and the two cherubs disappeared, and all was silent again. Gretta walked around the foyer, excited at the prospect of seeing Ben. She looked up at the countless figures carved into the ceiling and admired the wonderful workmanship. But eventually, her feet became heavy, and she could not stay awake. Exhausted from the long journey, she lay down on one stair and drifted off into a deep sleep.

Chapter 6
Celestial Heavens

When Gretta awoke from her sleep, she glanced at her watch and realized she had been sleeping on the stair for a long period of time. Feeling rested, she stood up and glanced around the gigantic foyer, amazed with its splendor. Her eyes gazed upwards once again to the high domed ceiling, magnificently crafted and painted with cherubs, angels, saints, apostles, and other heavenly beings. In the center of the domed ceiling was a gigantic, shimmering star that flashed like lightning. On both sides of the room were ivory stairwells with black wrought-iron railings. Above each stairwell was a huge chandelier that glittered with multicolored brilliant light. Giant white candles on the stairs burnt soft golden flames, and music played softly in the background. Yellow and white satin sofas were scattered around the foyer. A pink and white alabaster fountain on the right side of the foyer sprayed a fine mist of gold and white into the air. The sound of the mist was pleasing to the ears, and it had a calming effect on Gretta.

On the left side of the foyer was a grand hand-carved cedar and rosewood table, with one side resting against a wall. Its legs were shaped in subtle designs, and each leg had turquoise, red quartz, and white sapphire stones embedded in it. On the wall above the table hung a giant bronze and copper cross. A gentle breeze blew continuously throughout the foyer and opened pages of booklets on top of the table.

Gretta fell on her knees and bowed before the cross. Tears flowed constantly from her eyes. Suddenly, an angel dressed in pure white, with green leaves in his red hair, appeared.

He moved to Gretta and whispered in her ear, "Welcome to Celestial Heavens," and disappeared.

Gretta shook for several moments following the angel's appearance but soon regained her senses. She walked to the middle of the foyer and exclaimed out loud, "I'm in Celestial Heavens! I can't believe it! And I'm seeing angels. Oh, everything is so pristine."

She sat on the stairwell and was overawed by the atmosphere of peace in the air. After some time, a large dove with pink and white feathers appeared on the stairs and flew down along the railing and lightly brushed Gretta's right cheek. Then it came to rest on a giant, sparkling blue bell at the base of the left staircase. It cooed and beckoned to Gretta.

Slowly and hesitantly, she rose from the stairwell and walked over to the bell. She pulled a long silver cord attached to it, and bells started to ring. The bells chimed for several minutes, then all was silent.

Gretta gazed at the top of the right staircase and beheld an angel with six wings and soft flowing, flaxen hair, appear. He was dressed in bright red and held a golden sword in one hand. As he moved to the lower third of the staircase, a thick white cloud covered his feet and calves. The angel's presence livened the foyer. At length, he spoke, his voice sounding like clear, running water:

"You look very troubled and fearful. Fear not. For great news of joy abounds here: Ben Walker has arrived. Welcome, Gretta. I am the seraphim Liberate, an angelic being of the highest order associated with light, dedication, and purity. I continuously worship the Ancient of Days. As you notice, I have six wings – two to cover my face, two to cover my feet, and two to fly. I always fly above the throne of the Mighty One. You rang the bell, and Morningstar asked me to greet you. You were exhausted with the flight from planet earth, and right now you look very cold and hungry. Have a seat at the cedar and rosewood table, and I'll summon two cherubs to attend to you."

Try as she may, Gretta could not move from the spot where she stood. She was paralyzed with fear and stared in wonderment at the seraphim with the six wings.

Finally, she spoke, somewhat bewildered: "I am undone, because I am a being with unclean lips, and my friends and family are of unclean lips. How can I undo my situation?"

The seraphim reached into his belt and removed a live coal with one hand and laid it on Gretta's mouth.

"Lo, I have touched your lips, and your iniquity is no more. Come, sit at the table and prepare to eat."

Gretta moved slowly to the giant table while keeping her eyes fixed on the seraphim Liberate. The seraphim flared his wings, flew to the top of the staircase, and started to sing an ancient melody. The doorposts and the chandeliers began to shake, and the foyer was filled with white smoke. Then two chubby cherubs suddenly appeared on the lower stairwell and bowed to him. They had rosy, red cheeks, curly bronze-colored hair, and wore purple robes.

Seraphim Liberate spoke to them in a heavenly dialect and then addressed Gretta: "When you are finished eating, I will return. Adieu. I will see you later."

And he disappeared through the domed ceiling.

The two cherubs rushed about assembling a tray of refreshments and a pitcher of heavenly water from the sacred mountains. Within no time, the tray was in front of Gretta. One of the cherubs lifted the beleaguered visitor onto a giant carved chair near the table and placed her feet on a multicolored embroidered footstool. Then he wrapped Gretta in a soft green and white wool blanket.

At length, he spoke in a low, sonorous voice: "Eat now, my child. Once you are refreshed, seraphim Liberate will talk to you."

"Thank you," Gretta exclaimed. "Thank you for your kindness to me."

Quickly, she devoured several sugarcoated plum cakes, fresh fruit still covered with morning dew, and several loaves of golden bread stuffed with fresh fish. At length, Gretta felt satisfied, and the hunger pangs subsided. Seraphim Liberate appeared once again on the stairwell and walked slowly down the stairs toward Gretta. A small, thick white cloud rose from the lower half of the stairwell again, and eventually covered his lower legs.

His voice was as sweet as honey, and he beckoned to Gretta.

"This is as far as I come, dear one. You are still an earthly being and must eventually return to earth. I've been asked to minister to you and to enquire as to why you are here."

(The angel knew full well why she made the lengthy journey.)

Despite her fear, Gretta moved near the cloud covering the angel's lower legs and fell on her knees.

She raised her arms out to her and spoke in a quiet manner: "I came to enquire about Ben Walker's presence. You stated with great joy that he was here. I am ecstatic also that he is here. During his days on earth, he attended church whenever he could. He would state he was a stranger on earth and was passing through to be with Morningstar. However, I have some unfinished business with him. Hopefully, we can resolve it together. I'd like to see Ben now."

She began to cry softly again and fell prostrate before the angel. Seraphim Liberate held up his right hand and motioned for Gretta to stop crying.

Then he spoke, his voice sounding like a soft flute: "Ben Walker is currently having his vespers, and then will attend a session in preparation to meet Morningstar. I will allow a short visit, then you must return to earth."

She smiled graciously and added, "Ben used to sing in a choir when he resided with his mother in Louisville, Kentucky. He has offered to sing when he meets Morningstar. We are pleased and overjoyed with this kind gesture."

These thoughts stirred Gretta, and she replied, "I am so happy for Ben. At last, he has found true peace. His body is still flesh but is controlled by the Spirit. Now no more scabies or lice, no more infected feet, no crying, no pain, or sorrow. Poor Ben, he was in so much pain before he expired. Now he lives in a wonderful mansion he can call home. There are several issues I need to discuss with him – issues he didn't resolve before his passing. Perhaps, he and I can find a solution together."

Gretta was quiet now and fixed her gaze upon the angel. His face was shining like a brilliant diamond, and his wings moved back and forth with excitement.

The angel steadied himself on the stairs as he hummed a strain of music and then declared, with a sweet, mellow voice: "Ben Walker will be with you shortly. He has just finished his prayers and wishes to have a few moments to himself before seeing you. May your fellowship be sweet and memorable."

Then he bid Gretta adieu and disappeared into a cloud.

All was silent now in the foyer, and Gretta sat on the stair pondering the entire experience with the seraphim Liberate. Never had she seen such an amazing and beautiful creature who was so cordial and kind. As she thought of all the wondrous events that had just transpired, she suddenly felt nervous and anxious and wondered if perhaps she was in a trance.

"No," Gretta spoke to herself. "No, everything is very real, and I have met an angel, a seraph of the highest order."

Just then, a tall, black, muscular man appeared through a soft, billowy, pink cloud. He was wearing a white suit with silver pin-stripes and white alligator shoes. His black and silver hair was pulled back from his face and tied in a knot at the back of his neck. His body weight was in proportion to his build, and he wore diamond stud earrings and a sapphire ring on his index finger. In his right hand was a glistening silver and copper-tooled cane. Slowly, he went down the flight of steps until the white cloud surrounded his legs. It was Ben Walker.

He spoke in a deep, sweet-sounding voice: "My, my, what a pleasant surprise. Gretta, welcome. I certainly didn't expect to see you here yet. How kind and considerate of you. You worked so hard to save my life and did everything possible to help me recover. Thank you for your love and devotion to me. As you can see, I am a free man now. My glorified body is muscular and trim, and the barber and seamstress have worked wonders with me. This is a fabulous place to be, Gretta. There is no sorrow, no crying, no pain here. I have been asked to tap dance at a celebration for Morningstar. You didn't know that about me. Let me do a tap dance especially for you."

He clicked the heels of his white shoes on the white steps, and gestured and gyrated his body, arms, and legs back and forth with each tap. He hummed a tune as he danced and then whistled the last few bars. Gretta burst out laughing and tried to imitate him.

Finally, she cried out excitedly: "Oh, Ben, you look fantastic when you tap dance. If only your foot had not been injured the last few days of your earthly existence. I'm so pleased to see you among the angels and the great Morningstar. At first, I had doubts as to where your spirit and soul might be after you expired. A heavenly bird White Dove knew I had unfinished business with you and offered to fly me here. I see you're walking about, and you no longer have an infected foot."

Ben listened intently to Gretta, gave a slight bow, then laughed.

"You say there is unfinished business to discuss with me? Before we get to that, I want to let you in on a big secret, Miss Gretta. It's because of you I'm in heaven."

Gretta's facial expression went to one of complete shock, and she moved slowly up the stairs within inches of the white cloud. Somewhat vexed and feeling angry inside, she raised her voice and snapped at him.

"I don't understand. I never did anything to hurt you, and now you're saying I'm the reason you're in heaven. What kind of nonsense is that?"

Ben chuckled and then smiled winningly.

"My, it's good to laugh. Let me tell you how I came to reside in this place."

Briefly, Ben told Gretta how he tried to catch her attention at BacNauld's Bar one day and how a potted plant fell on his foot. The rest was history, and she knew every detail following.

"I'm here because of you, Gretta. I wouldn't change my place for anything."

Gretta was bewildered and filled with jealousy and went down the stairs. She paced back and forth in the foyer, mulling over what Ben had just told her. Mixed emotions swirled in her mind. Why hadn't he told her about this while on earth? Was she really the cause of his injured left foot and his following death? She felt a stab in her heart, and for a moment became lightheaded and dizzy. Gretta grabbed onto the cedar and rosewood table and steadied herself.

Angrier and more envious now, she turned and gave an icy reply: "Ben, I'd give anything to change places with you. Oh, that it would have been me with the injured foot instead of you. I think you are surprised by joy, and now you are truly content."

"Yes, I am filled with peace and joy. I have no pain, and I can walk. But I find you anxious and upset with me. I think we'll go to the unfinished business you wish to discuss. What are the issues?"

Gretta spoke up sharp and quick: "First, you should have made the phone call with me to the Housing and Apartment Bureau about Nigglewood Convalescent. You would have met Mr. John Dicton who is now investigating the premises. Second, I went to look for you among the various beach shelters, but you were nowhere to be found. If you had gone to the hospital when we last met, you may still be alive today. Third, who is going to tell your mother and Lise that you have passed away? I'm sure you haven't spoken to either for some time. Finally, there's me. I don't feel responsible for not waving to you at BacNauld's Bar, and I certainly am not responsible for the flowerpot falling on your foot. That's your problem. I forgive you for these troubling events, but

I can't forget them. You have no idea what agony I feel in my heart at this moment."

A feeling of compassion came over Ben, and he felt his eyes moisten with tears.

Tenderly, he piped up: "I don't know what to say, Gretta. You ask me to account for all those issues. I was too sick and in pain my last few days on earth to make a call with you to the Housing Bureau or meet Mr. Dicton. I should have gone to the hospital the last time I saw you, but I didn't. I think my foot infection was beyond any help from a hospital. The relationship between my daughter and her mother is difficult now for, but I think I can still make amends with them, even from here."

Ben gazed warmly at Gretta and continued, his voice sounding like a deep, soft note of a country-church bell.

"We have a short period of time left before you return to earth. You will be returning to the intensive care. Could you call my mother and tell her the sad news that I have expired? She will be heartbroken at first. But when you tell her you saw me in heaven, she will be ecstatic and want to know more. I have a letter for her and would like to ask you to mail it for me. I've asked her forgiveness for my being so calloused and uncaring. Mother will love the stationary. It's made of fine woven lamb's wool with gold etching around the border. A small emerald and diamond jewel are imbedded in the right-hand corner. Such a gesture will stir and remind her she's not forgotten on the long, lonely journey of mourning that lies ahead."

Gretta stood in the middle of the foyer and stared at Ben. His face and whole being were shining like the sun. Finally, she held her head erect and moved with new assurance.

Begrudgingly, she replied: "Yes, of course. When I return to the intensive care, I will call her myself, and tell of your tragic death and journey to Celestial Heavens in a chariot accompanied by angels. I will then tell her I went to see you in the heavens and about the dialogue we had. She will be very saddened at first but will be touched by your new home, a beautiful pink mansion. Moreover, she will ask me about Morningstar and your unlimited freedom in seeing him. I'll tell her about the letter you wrote and will ask her to keep a sharp eye for it in the mail. What about your daughter, Lise?"

"I have also written a letter to her but will have angel Liberate deliver it to her. A heavenly intervention is needed to shake my offspring out of her rebellious, stubborn attitude. Mother's letter is on the table to your right. I have one last request. I have a jewel box of precious and semiprecious stones for Mother as well. Could I ask you to send it to her?"

"Certainly." Gretta consented, her voice tremulous.

Ben gazed at Gretta fondly and pondered his past friendship with her. The cloud that clothed his legs and feet started to move slowly to the top of the stairwell taking Ben with it. Ben realized the time had come to part with Gretta.

He spoke with an undertone of melancholy: "Gretta, someday you will be with me in Celestial Heavens meeting Morningstar. We will dance on the golden streets, sing by the crystal waters, and shout songs of joy. You are a rare jewel and are still called to serve your patients on earth, bringing hope, healing, and meaning in life. Nursing allows you to achieve so much good. Be patient and continue your work in the community. Morningstar is coming sooner than you think! What a magnificent day that will be! Then you will be with me forever."

Ben tap danced on the step of the stairwell once again, and Gretta did wildly exciting body movements. She called out to him.

"Thank you, Ben. I will do my part on earth. Then I will see you and Morningstar in heaven. Oh!"

Her face had a glimmer of exuberance off and on.

"Goodbye, Gretta. Remember to support widows, orphans, and the homeless. Cherish your patients. Desire wisdom. Honor your father and mother. Ponder those things of good report – honesty, integrity, and purity. Adieu, Gretta."

Angel Liberate appeared now beside Ben, blew a trumpet, and the two slowly faded away into the fluffy pink cloud. A thick blanket of white clouds now covered the stairwell and sprayed a fine mist into the foyer. The air became cooler, and a brisk breeze started to swirl around the room. It increased in velocity until suddenly White Dove appeared and quietly landed next to Gretta. The agile bird hovered over her with its wings, then lifted the girl onto its back. She nestled into its soft feathers, and within the twinkling of an eye, they were outside the mansion in the clear blue sky.

The bird with its passenger moved quickly to planet earth, passing through a thick pall of mushroom-like gray clouds until it entered a sky that was pitch-black. A few stars twinkled dimly in the night, and the moon glowed a cold icy blue. The temperature was freezing, and soon they encountered a torrential rainstorm. The dove pressed on undeterred by the perilous conditions. Several hawks and cruel-eyed black birds tried to grab the dove and Gretta for prey, but the clever bird slipped effortlessly through their evil grasp. As soon as they neared planet earth, loud noises, sirens, and shouting could be heard in the streets. Multicolored city lights blinked on and off over a vast landscape of houses, trees, boulevards, and commercial buildings. The dove circled over Nigglewood Convalescent Manor, gave a grunt of disapproval, then flew onto Walston Hospital.

As soon as the hospital appeared, the dove made a loud squawk, then descended for landing. The wind was blowing fiercely, and puddles of rainwater were scattered about the rooftop. The dove landed in a large amount of water but passed through it quickly. The bird with its passenger made its way through corridors, elevators, and business offices until it arrived at room 3336 of the intensive care. Nurses and attendants were busy in their rooms, alarms were sounding on and off, and pleasant chatter from the doctors could be heard in the background.

Room 3336 was exactly as they had left it. It was obvious the day nurse had not cleaned it. The ventilator and intravenous pumps were pushed to one side, but the continuous dialysis machine was still attached to Ben. The used code cart was empty of its stock, and the trash cans and linen hampers were overflowing. The large, deceased body lay half naked under the green cooling blanket. A faucet was still running in the bathroom, and the room telephone rang continuously.

The dove circled the room, lowered Gretta gently into a chair, and cooed softly to her. Then it disappeared into the night. Gretta stared at Ben's lifeless body and was overwhelmed with sadness. Finally, she rose from the chair, made her way to the corpse, and sat next to him. Then she bowed her head and wept.

Chapter 7
Finale

"Gretta, Gretta, I've been calling you for the last twenty minutes. Why, whatever is the matter? You look so brokenhearted and mournful. Your face is swollen and covered in tear stains. I know you were attached to Ben, but I didn't think his death would upset you this much. Can I be of help?" exclaimed the tall, husky nurse.

She was near five feet eight inches with tousled brown hair and sparkling brown eyes, and she was wearing a bright-blue printed uniform. Her black and white pointed rhinestone-studded glasses gave her a retro look.

Gretta rose from the lifeless body and spoke in a low-pitched voice filled with intense sadness: "Yes, Mirabel, there is something you can do. Could you start to clean up the room? It's a mess – used and dirty equipment are everywhere. The day nurse was to begin tidying and disinfecting after the arrest, but I guess that didn't happen. I'll help you wrap the body shortly. I must inform the mother of Ben's passing. Someone else from Celestial Heavens will inform the daughter, Lise."

The comment about the heavens stirred Mirabel, and she stared at Gretta with her dark yet bright eyes.

She said lightly: "Celestial Heavens? What's that? I'll start to clean up right now. But you weren't here, Gretta? We've been looking for you everywhere. Some of the staff were thinking of calling 911 and filing a missing person's report."

Gretta gave a gentle smile, and the sadness dissipated from her face momentarily.

"Let's say I went to visit Ben. I've been with him all this time."

"Well, I'll be a monkey's uncle. I've never heard of a nurse going to visit a deceased patient after a cardiac arrest. There's so much work to do after a

"

death and so little time to finish it. Tell me," she whispered with a slight giggle. "Did you see my deceased brother? He must be playing the banjo up there; Music was his passion while he was on earth. I miss him dearly. He died in a traffic accident three years ago."

Mirabel's face went melancholy, and she backed away from the corpse. Gretta placed one arm around her and gave the nurse a warm hug.

"I'm sorry your brother passed away in such a violent manner. I can't say that I saw him, but I did see Ben, numerous angels, a seraph, doves, lush greenery, beautiful multicolored mansions – all in all, a wonderful paradise. Now there's a lot to do. I must call the organ donor hotline. Someone may be the recipient of a harvested organ. Did anyone call the mother and inform her of Ben's death while I was away?"

Mirabel pointed to the phone.

"It's already been done. I called the organ donor hotline while you were supposedly in heaven. Ben was too septic for any organs to be harvested for transplant. He didn't take care of himself. Every microbe possible was in his blood. As to the mother, the NOR called her several times, but there was no answer."

"Thank you so much, Mirabel. I must call Mrs. Walker now and inform her of the death. I'll be with you shortly."

While Mirabel went to work removing the lines and tubes from Ben's body, Gretta walked to a small sitting room and sat in a recliner. She closed her eyes for several minutes, and once again imagined the scenario in heaven. Those were divine moments of bliss, and she coveted the day when she and Ben would be together again. Yes, she would tap-dance with him on the golden streets and sing songs by the crystal sea. But she was on earth now, and Ben's mother needed to be reckoned with and told he was deceased.

She paused to think of his daughter Lise and soliloquized to herself: "Surely, a daughter would want to know if her father had passed away. No wonder Ben didn't send her any mail. She was rude, nasty, and very rebellious. I'm surprised she even spoke to him in the past. The angel Liberate will have to speak to her and tell of his passing. There's no question about that. I hope his mother will be more cooperative. I must get her phone number from the NOR."

Gretta rose from the chair and walked to an isolation room where the NOR, gowned and gloved, was assisting in a procedure. She was busy in the room for another hour, so Gretta decided to look one more time at the face sheet in the nurse's record. There was no number there, so she decided to call Nigglewood Convalescent. It was now three forty-five, a God forsaken hour to call anyone. Hastily, she dialed the manor and anxiously waited for someone to answer. The telephone rang six times before a soft, low, velvety voice was heard on the other end:

"Nigglewood Convalescent Manor, this is Grenadine speaking. How may I help you?"

"Ma'am, I'm Gretta, a nurse from Walston Hospital. Mr. Ben Walker passed away several hours ago in the intensive care. I must call his mother and tell her the sad news, but I don't have her telephone number. Would you have it in your personal records?"

"Oh," replied the weary-eyed employee, shocked with the news. "I'm sorry to hear he passed away. I know he wasn't well recently. Let me see. We have five Walkers here at Nigglewood. Ah, here he is. Ben's mother's name is Hestor Walker, and she resides in Memphis, Tennessee. According to our records, she last saw him five years ago. Her telephone number is 607-992-8181. Please give my condolences to her."

"I will do that, Grenadine. Thank you for the number."

The phone clicked lightly as Gretta put the receiver down. She stood quietly, deep in thought, her hand resting on the phone.

Another nurse approached her and asked, "Are you all right, Gretta? You look very upset, tired, and weary. May I help you?"

"No," she replied remorsefully. "Calling a relative at three forty-five in the morning can be difficult. I need a little time before I call Ben's mother. I'm sure she's deep in sleep."

Finally, she dialed Hestor's telephone number and waited for it to ring. It seemed endless moments passed before a shrill sound was heard on the other end. Brr. Strong, slow, and long, eight to ten times it rang before the elderly black woman finally awoke from her sleep.

The air in the bedroom was cold and crisp, and the old lady shivered in the chilliness of the early morning. Hestor Walker reached for a brown and gold throw at the end of the bed and wrapped it around her orange-colored nightie and black wool jacket. She adjusted the black velvet ruffled nightcap on her head and then peered into the pitch darkness of her bedroom. After approximately thirty seconds, she saw the alarm clock on the night table and groped for it.

"Why, it's only three fifty-five in the mornin'. Who's callin' at this God-forsaken hour?" she muttered to herself "It's probably another crank call. I hate calls like that. I'll wait here. Maybe the ringin' will stop. I don't want to get up for nothin'. The bedroom is too chilly for that."

But the telephone continued to ring nonstop. Finally, the disheveled woman rose from the bed, tightened the throw around her, grabbed her black lacquer cane with the ivory handle, and hobbled to the phone at snail's pace.

"Hello," replied a deep, slow-speaking, throaty voice. The weary-eyed individual tried several times to clear her pharynx from oral secretions.

"Ma'am, this is Walston Hospital in Los Angeles, California. I wish to speak to Hestor Walker."

"Her speakin," sounded the sleepy, sonorous voice, somewhat perturbed and hesitant.

"Hestor, my name is Gretta. I'm a nurse at Walston Hospital. I have some bad news to convey to you. Your son Ben Walker passed away several hours ago from a serious blood infection and a gangrenous foot. Our sincere condolences to you and from the staff of Nigglewood Convalescent."

Gretta choked back her tears and prepared for Hestor's reaction. First, there was nothing verbal on the phone, but she could hear furniture being struck by something with a deafening sound.

She was curious and asked: "What's that noise in the background? It sounds like something is being hit."

There was no response to her question. Then she heard a burst of loud uncontrollable sobs. After several minutes of sobbing, Hestor sat down in a chair with a loud thump and stared into the darkness. Her dark-brown button eyes continually swelled with tears, and she pulled a well-used red handkerchief from her bosom and blew her stuffed-up nose. When she had sufficiently recovered from the impact of the news, she took the phone again in her hands.

"Oh, oh … my only son, Gretta. He was my one and only son. Oh … this is a very sad and painful day. If I wasn't sittin' down, I would faint on the floor. I'm sorry I lost it for several minutes. My heart is throbbin' with pain, and my heartbeat is rapid and poundin'. The grief is too much to bear. My only son … he is gone. And I'm all alone. When I spoke to him on the phone in the past, I always encouraged him to see a doctor on a yearly basis. He was on blood pressure medication and was a borderline diabetic. His heart needed some tendin' too. An infected foot? How did he get that? He never had problems with his feet before."

Gretta felt put on the spot momentarily. She knew very well why Ben's foot was gangrenous. Yet she didn't feel now was the time to share details.

After pausing briefly, she replied, "I'm pleased you were concerned about his health, Hestor. Towards the end of his life, he struggled with his blood pressure and heart rate, and his sugars were elevated. He didn't want meal service from the outside. He preferred to eat at BacNauld's Bar and Grill, and unfortunately, the food there was high in sugar and carbohydrates. With his sugar elevated, he was a prime candidate for a serious infection."

Hestor became indignant with the last remark and retorted, "An elevated sugar wouldn't cause a gangrenous foot. There must be another reason."

Gretta sidestepped the point and continued: "Hestor, it is a sad day for all of us, but I have some good news to share. Ben is alive in Celestial Heavens. I went to see him there, and we had a wonderful visit. He was preparing for a welcome dinner with Morningstar and looked in fine form. He was 150 pounds, wearing a beautiful white suit and matching shoes, and was walking with a glistening silver and copper-tooled cane. He tap danced for me to a heavenly tune. It was awesome!"

Hestor was astonished by what Gretta had just told her. She reached for a clean handkerchief from a night table, blew her stuffed-up nose once again, then remarked: "This is a real surprise. You say you went to see Ben? Why, I've never heard of such a thing. Are the rates expensive? If not, I may go there myself."

She leaned back into the chair and sighed with wonderment. The stream of tears had lessened somewhat, and Hestor dabbed her puffy chipmunk cheeks from time to time.

"The journey is free, Hestor."

"I do believe you, Gretta. I do believe you. However, I'm so sad now. My one and only son is no longer here. I can't tell you how my heart is achin'."

"Well, I have something special for you. Ben gave me a letter, handwritten by himself, addressed to his loving mother who still abides on earth. He also sent a small jewel box of precious and semi-precious stones, especially for you."

Hestor gave a gasp and instantly became interested in the letter and jewel box.

"Oh," she exclaimed. "There's a letter? Please open and read it to me. The jewel box you can send by mail. What does it look like?"

"I'll tell you about the jewel box after I read the letter. The letter is most important."

"Please read the letter now," replied the grief-stricken woman. "I'm curious what he wrote."

Gretta opened the letter, and the diamond and emerald stones in the right upper hand corner sparkled brilliantly in the light.

She began to read through tears of joy:

"My dearest darling, Mother,

So much has happened since I last spoke to you, and I'm ashamed of the lapse of time between us. As you know, I resided at Nigglewood Convalescent Manor in Los Angeles for the last six years and spent some time in Walston Hospital fighting disease and infection as old age touched me. When not in the hospital, I spent my time encouraging and helping the men and women of the manor, hoping the situation would improve. However, our efforts were often ineffective. The care remained substandard, and the meals frequently never reached us. The rooms were rarely cleaned, the laundry wasn't done for a month, and cockroaches were everywhere. As I watch from heaven, I can only hope and pray that their plight improves with time.

My last remaining days on earth were spent in the hospital. My dear nurse, Gretta, did everything possible to restore me to health. Unfortunately, I was too weak to 'fight the fight', and entered the valley of the shadow of death December 7 at 2100. I was immediately transported to a marvelous home by a myriad of angels and a fiery chariot. They have not ceased to minister to me since my arrival. I am being groomed to meet Morningstar shortly and can hardly wait for that moment.

You would love to see me now, Mother.

I'm back to my youthful weight of 150 pounds, and I look great! I've started to dance again, and I'm told I will be dancing for the welcome dinner. I'm sure by now you are asking what responsibilities I have as a new arrival. Well, believe it or not, I will be greeting the newcomers as they enter the heavens. There will be a short period of time for sleep. Upon arising, I will say my prayers, go to the library to read an epistle or psalm, then possibly see a video on a major event.

I may also partake in a singsong. Following that, I will eat a small meal and then start work.

I know you are a real Trojan when it comes to reading the Word, but I must share a sacred moment with you. Last night, when I arrived, Elijah's chariot appeared in the sky, carrying an evangelist and his wife. Elijah, the horses, and the chariot were etched in flaming fire but not consumed by it. He rolled on to the golden streets, and angels everywhere shouted with ecstasy. There is so much to tell you Mother, and I can't wait until you join me.

Enclosed you will find in the upper right-hand corner of the writing paper a one-carat diamond and a two-carat emerald – both birthstones as you know. The diamond is for you, and the emerald is for my daughter, Lise.

Lise and I have had a very strained relationship these past few years. Could you call and tell her the precious stone is from me? May it release love tones within her. Care for her, dear mother, just as you cared for me.

I must sign off now. I need to learn some new songs for the welcome banquet and practice my tap dancing. Morningstar expects the best from us. Mother, until we meet again, may you remain steadfast and filled with peace. You are precious and the apple of my eye. Be good to Gretta. Take up the task of comforting and helping those left behind at Nigglewood. There is much work to be done there. May the Spirit establish and strengthen you after you have grieved a short while.

Your heavenly son,
Ben Walker."

New life surged through Hestor's old dry bones, and she had an outburst of joy.

She shouted with surprise, "Gretta, this is the best news comin' my way in a long time. I'm still very sad with my son's passin', but after years of intercessory prayer, my son has made it into heaven. Glory, Hallelujah!"

She sang a Negro spiritual, then spoke into the phone again, "I feel the Lord is sayin' to me, 'O dry bones, hear d' Word of d' Lord.' Lord God is speakin' to me right now. He is breathin' on me and touchin' me. I know he is the Lord just as Ezekiel knew him. And Ezekiel prophesied when the Israelites had lost their vision from God; I too had lost my vision that Ben would be in heaven. But, dear Gretta, you have seen him, and now my bones are rattlin' with joy. O dry bones, hear d' Word of d' Lord."

Hestor pulled off the small black velvet nightcap from her head and twirled it around one finger while she sang a victory tune.

When she was finished singing, she continued in her old voice: "Gretta – what's the diamond like? I think it would look nice as a brooch. And the jewel box? Describe it to me."

The atmosphere became more carefree, and Gretta's voice sounded friendlier with a soft fluting quality.

"The diamond would look nice as a brooch. It is marquis-shaped and glitters constantly with an icy blue-white glow. The emerald is just as radiant and is slightly larger than the diamond. The jewel box is heart-shaped and is eighteen karat gold. Precious and semiprecious stones decorate the front and the sides. It is stunning."

"Ah," Hestor sighed. "God knows how to give perfect gifts to his loved ones. Well, I'll be out to see you soon, Gretta. I have a few things to tidy up here. Oh, I can't wait to see you."

Hestor rose from the old chair and turned on a lampstand light nearby. However, waves of anger passed through her as she thought of Ben's neglect and abuse. A fiery passion burnt inside her for the underprivileged in care facilities everywhere.

She stomped her foot on the floor and muttered out loud: "So, all this time Ben was at Nigglewood, they've been abusin' him. Well, they ain't going to do that anymore, Gretta. Change is comin'. I'm going to file a formal complaint with the health authorities once I get to Los Angeles. They've tangled with the wrong lady."

Hestor was in a fuming rage now and hit various pieces of furniture once again with her cane. This time, she stomped the floor several times with both feet without delay.

"I'm with you, Hestor. I have some ideas about changing the care facility for the better. There will be a new cafeteria with fruits, yoghurt, vegetables, and every type of nut. The rooms will be serviced by attendants who are dressed in colorful attire. Fresh water will be provided daily, the sheets will be changed weekly, the carpets kept clean. On the second floor will be a custom-made library –something completely new and different. It will have newspapers, magazines, journals, and books. The front foyer will be circular and have plants and small shrubs around it. The top floor will be a sundeck and will have chairs and tables for inhabitants and guests. Just let me know the date and time of your airplane arrival. I'll meet you at the airport. Nigglewood Convalescent is in for a real surprise. I don't know how Ben survived it there. The latter part of the year, he basically lived elsewhere. He spent most nights in a shelter on the beach."

Hestor let out a loud shriek.

"Enough is enough! I'll be dealing with that. Trust me. Your plans for the facility are very interesting. I need some time to think about it before I comment."

Gretta glanced at her watch and saw it was almost five o'clock. She knew it was time to close the conversation.

"I have two things to say before I part with you. First, I have a secret regarding Ben's foot, but I will tell you about that when you are here. Second, you won't forget to call Lise and tell her about the emerald stone?"

"A secret regarding Ben's foot? I guess I'll have to wait 'till I see you. I will call Lise and tell her about the emerald jewel. That child has terrible manners. Just like her mother. If she doesn't want it, I'll keep it. Two brooches are better than one, you know."

Hestor gave a hearty laugh, then talked about her flight plans, places to see, restaurants, and her up-and-coming meeting with the Health Authorities. Gretta promised a full day at the downtown market and the garment district.

****

"Gretta, the attendant from the morgue is here. Could you help him? Are Ben's mortuary papers completed?"

****

"Gretta, have you called housekeeping yet? It's getting late. They're anxious to bring the emergency admission before seven o'clock."

****

Gretta moved to a quiet area and spoke for the last time, "I've got to go. They're calling me to duty. Tell me you'll do something especially for Ben and me while you're still in Tennessee. The next time you're in a restaurant, stand up and ask the guests for your attention. Tell them your son is in heaven and is having fellowship with the great Morningstar. Let them rise and applaud. Share the celebration with them."

"I'll do just that, my beloved nurse. We'll also do that in Los Angeles. We'll raise the roof. Until we meet again, stay well. Goodbye."

Click. The phone went dead.

"Gretta, are you deaf? The morgue attendant has been waiting thirty minutes for you. Please try to hurry."

"Gretta, the emergency nurse is on the phone now and wants to give a report on your patient."

"Gretta ..."

"Gretta ..."